Susannah and the Poison Green HALLOWEEN

Also by Patricia Elmore:
Susannah and the Blue House Mystery

Susannah and the Poison Green HALLOWEEN

Patricia Elmore

SCHOLASTIC INC.
New York Toronto London Auckland Sydney

For Tom, my brother and oldest friend,
and Lee, the sister I always wanted.

My thanks, for their generous help, to:
Margarita Dorland, L.V.N., and Steve Rubin,
for researching medical facts; Judith Serin and
Marcia Amsterdam, for editing the first drafts;
and Harriett Kirk and Susan Clymer,
for very helpful advice.

ISBN 0-590-43471-3

 Published by Scholastic Inc., 730 Broadway, New York, NY 10003, by arrangement with Dutton's Children's Books, a division of Penguin Books USA Inc.

12 11 10 9 8 7 6 5 4 3 2 1 0 1 2 3 4 5/9

Printed in the U.S.A. 40

First Scholastic printing, October 1990

1

Even before anybody got poisoned and the police started grilling us about the Eucalyptus Arms, that Halloween was a bummer. To begin with, when I went to the girls' bathroom to change for the school parade, I discovered I'd brought the bag with the trash instead of the one with my costume.

"Oh well," said Susannah, "at least you'll be the only one in the parade dressed as a Safeway grocery bag."

Susannah raced home with me after school to get my costume. But I couldn't find it anywhere.

"Pop, have you seen my costume?"

"No, Lucy. Oh." He looked up from his newspaper. "It wasn't that bag of rags and tinfoil you left on the kitchen table, was it?"

I wouldn't have described my costume in quite those words, but I *had* left it on the kitchen table.

"Gee, princess, I thought that was just junk and I was cleaning up, so — "

"You threw away my costume?" I shrieked and

raced out back to the garbage cans.

Pop followed. "Princess, I'm afraid they've already taken the garbage away. I'm so sorry — I — "

I stalked back to my room and flung myself on my bed. So much for Halloween. No costume, no treats, no party, no nothing. "I wonder what's on TV tonight."

Susannah patted my shoulder. "You can find something to wear. Maybe your father's got an old suit."

"No! I want to be the Death Queen of the planet Morticia, like I planned."

"The *who*?" Susannah doesn't read comics much.

"The Death Queen," I sniffed, "is this cruel ruler of the planet Morticia who's always plotting weird ways to kill people, only Captain Terran saves them. She's kind of beautiful in a cold way, except her skin is green."

I sighed, thinking how I'd have looked slinking along in my silver-spangled black cape, smiling wickedly, my skin a gruesome green and my hair hidden under a black turban with a silver skull in the center. I'd wasted half a roll of foil cutting out that skull.

"Sounds sweet," Susannah said drily, "but better settle for something less depraved if we're going trick-or-treating today. Grandpa's picking us up here at six for my party."

I swiped my nose with my fist. "I can't go to the party. Not after telling everybody what a great costume I was going to have."

"Huh!" Susannah turned to the door. "Lucy, I thought you had more guts. Well, enjoy TV while I'm trick-or-treating."

There are times when I could gleefully murder Susannah, even if she is my best friend. At such moments I wonder how I, Lucy the Slugger, ever got mixed up with the Brains of Washington School. Sometimes I even wonder if Susannah and I shouldn't have stayed enemies as we once were. And this was definitely one of those moments.

"Susannah Higgins, you wait for me or I'll never speak to you again." I jumped up and began looking for something to turn into a costume. "I suppose I *could* cut eyeholes in the sheet and go as just a dumb old ghost," I said.

"If you don't mind sleeping with your toes poking through afterwards."

"So I'll wear socks to bed." Snatching off the sheet, I cut out two holes. But when I got the sheet on, one of the eyeholes was over my left ear.

"You might try stretching your face," Susannah said solemnly.

"Dry up." She could talk, wearing that neat outfit her grandparents brought back from their vacation in Africa. "Hand me the scissors."

I cut out one big circle for my head. Now I could

make up my face as I'd planned for my role as Death Queen of the planet Morticia. I'd look scarier and see better, too.

I'd just finished cutting when Pop walked in and thrust a package at me.

"This is all they had left at the discount store, princess. Hope it will do."

It was a Little Bo Peep costume, complete with plastic crook.

Frankly, I preferred the sheet. Little Bo Peep just isn't my style. But I couldn't hurt Pop's feelings.

"Gee." I choked. "You shouldn't have done it." I meant that.

Pop looked relieved. "You really like it? I was afraid you'd think it was a bit — well, young. You deserve a real costume for once. I haven't bought you one in a long time."

When Pop was gone, I squirmed into the costume — it was a tight fit — and mournfully studied myself in the mirror while Susannah struggled to keep a straight face.

"Ar-r-rgh!" I snarled. "Well, maybe I won't run into somebody like Knievel Jones. But I can't go to your party like — "

There in the doorway stood Carla Able, the last person next to Knievel that I wanted to see.

"Oh, is *that* your costume, Lucy?" she asked sweetly.

Carla was new in our class and lived a few blocks away in the Eucalyptus Arms Apartments, where her stepfather was the manager. At school she hung around with Susannah and me. Not that we asked her to, but Susannah wouldn't tell anybody to buzz off. Oh, Carla was okay, I guess, only sometimes she got on my nerves. Always whining. I'd forgotten she'd invited herself along tonight.

Carla eyed me disdainfully. "I thought you said your costume was something special."

"It is." Thinking fast, I grabbed a tube of green makeup I'd bought at Woolworth's for my Death Queen costume. "Just watch. See, everybody thinks I'm sweet Little Bo Peep till I tear off my mask" — I smeared the green goop over my face — "then behold: the Death Queen of the planet Morticia."

Not a bad idea, come to think of it. Anyway, Carla looked impressed.

"Where's *your* costume, Carla?" Susannah asked as I smeared black mascara above my eyes.

"That's what I came to tell you. Mama's taking me to buy it now. So you'll have to wait for me."

Wait for her? While everybody else was stuffing their treat bags?

"Look," I said, "you'll catch up with us somewhere. Anyway, you'll see us at Susannah's party."

Carla's eyelids tightened. "*I'd* wait for *you.*"

"*Sure* you would," I scoffed.

Carla turned to Susannah. "Please wait. It's all Nadine's fault. Mama spent all her money on stupid Nadine's stupid dress for a stupid high school dance, so there wasn't any left for my costume till my stepfather got paid today — "

"Why didn't you make a costume?" asked Susannah. "That's the best kind."

"Really," I sighed, staring down at my store-bought one.

"It is?" Carla looked doubtful. "Then maybe I should have let Mama make mine, like she wanted to. But anyway, she was too busy yesterday, fixing this big dinner. Some big deal, just because Nadine's social worker was coming. Even Nadine stirred her lazy bones to make dessert."

"Social worker?" Susannah peered curiously over her glasses. "How come your sister has a social worker?" Susannah always thinks like a detective.

Carla looked mysterious. "I'm not supposed to tell, but Nadine got in bad trouble a couple of years ago — drugs and stuff. They only let her go home because they thought she was really sick. Nadine's good at faking."

"Well, go on," I urged. "How did she get in trouble?"

Carla smirked. "Wait for me and I'll tell you when I get back."

"No deal." I wasn't *that* curious. "We're going trick-or-treating *now*. Ready, Susannah?"

For a minute I thought Carla might smash me one, but Susannah stepped between us. "Tell you what, Carla, you go get your costume while we work this neighborhood — No, listen, will you?

We'll collect your treats and meet you later. That way you'll make out better than if we wait for you."

Carla thought it over. "Okay. Meet me at my place, the basement apartment of the Eucalyptus Arms — you know where. Promise?"

"Promise." Susannah checked her watch. "We'll be there at five-thirty. And tell your mother you can ride with us to my party. Grandpa's picking us up at six here at Lucy's."

"And you better be there on time," I yelled as Carla dashed off.

That's how it happened that, at nearly five-thirty on Halloween evening, Susannah and I walked up to the Eucalypus Arms Apartments, our bags already heavy with goodies. Now begins the part the police questioned us about over and over. For it was someone in the Eucalyptus Arms who gave us the poisoned candy.

2

"Why did they name it the Eucalyptus Arms?" I asked when we arrived just before five-thirty. With that name, you'd expect it to be in a forest of eucalyptus trees, not jammed up to the sidewalk with a scrawny palm tree in front. An ugly, green concrete slab, it stood at the end of a row of cozy old frame houses with petunias still blooming in their yards. "Looks more like the Putrified Arms to me."

"That's a poisonous shade of green, all right," Susannah agreed. "They must have scraped it off a tomb."

Speaking of tomb scrapings, a vampire hurtled around the corner and nearly slammed into us.

"Are you a *real* vampire?" I demanded.

He slavered juicily and asked my blood type.

"Oh good," I said, "I was afraid you might be Knievel Jones."

"Yeah?" The vampire licked his fangs. "Well, there's only one girl dumb enough to wear a costume like *that*. Little Bo Peep!" He doubled over laughing.

I threatened him with my crook, but it caught on my sleeve and twisted into a U. "Laugh it up, fang face. When I shove those plastic teeth down your throat, we'll see what's funny."

Susannah groaned. "Oh, no. Have I got to referee this match?"

But then the door of the Eucalyptus Arms opened, and breaking off his laughter, Knievel dived through it. Following, I found him uprighting a tiny Superman and mumbling, "Sorry, kid."

"You big bully!" snarled the mother as she snatched Superman away.

Knievel stared after them, muttering, then shrugged. "Let's get moving. Five-thirty and I haven't even started." He darted down the hall while Susannah and I took the stairs to the basement where Carla lived.

I thought we were rid of him, but no such luck. As we rang the bell under the sign MANAGER, there was a rush of feet behind us and Knievel skidded into me. Next thing I knew he was poking a finger down the back of my collar.

"Hold it, Lucy. Dropped my fangs down your neck."

I fished them out. "Here, put them in quick before you scare somebody. They make you look almost human."

A peephole opened in the door. "Oh, not more kids."

"Thick or theet!" answered Knievel, jamming the plastic teeth into place.

"We're friends of Carla's," Susannah explained. "Is she here?"

A thin teenager in a bathrobe opened the door a crack. I decided she must be Nadine. "Carla's out with my mother. Sorry, no treats — my mother's bringing some back." She started to close the door.

Knievel shoved a foot into the crack. "What do you mean you got no treats?" He peered inside. "What's that on that plate?" Worming past her, he pulled out a plate of cookies from the shelf under the end table.

"Oh, so *there's* where I put those granola bars last night," said Nadine. "Trust a pig to find food. Sure, take them. They're probably stale by now anyway. Just hurry up, will you? I've got to get dressed. Kids!" she sniffed as if she'd never been one.

"Tell Carla we came," Susannah said as I grabbed two granola bars for us before they followed the other four into Knievel's bag. "We'll wait around awhile, but if she's much later, tell Carla to meet us at Lucy's."

"Sure, sure, I'll tell her — if I'm still here." Nadine closed the door on us.

I was about to follow Knievel upstairs when Susannah caught my arm.

"Hold it. We promised Carla, and it's only a

couple of minutes after five-thirty now." She glanced at her watch.

"Yeah, but we could wait upstairs where there's more light."

"And more apartments to trick-or-treat, of course?" Susannah grinned. "Well, we did promise our folks not to go off into any dark, lonely places, and this hall *is* dark."

"Besides, we'll do Carla a favor to collect her treat from the Candy Lady before she's cleaned out."

The Candy Lady on the first floor was famous in the neighborhood. I'd heard about her even before Carla moved in. Word gets around fast about somebody who gives kids candy or cookies whenever they knock at her door. Her real name was Mrs. Sweet, which suited her perfectly.

Tonight she had large chocolate cupcakes with green icing. Knievel was wolfing down his when we arrived.

"You're just in time." Mrs. Sweet handed us the last two on the plate. "Now all I have left are the ones I made specially for Carla and the boy upstairs." When we explained about Carla, she gave us hers, too — an extra large one with her name iced on it.

Knievel's fangs drooled. "Don't you have one more? That's the best thing I ever ate. Fudge, nuts — it's got everything."

Mrs. Sweet laughed. "I can't resist flattery.

Here, take the one I made for the little boy upstairs. He won't be home for a few days anyway."

Knievel jammed the cupcake into his mouth with a grunt of thanks as he raced to the next door. I resisted the urge to do the same, knowing I'd hate myself if I arrived stuffed at Susannah's party. I put the green cupcake into my bag. Normally, of course, I don't eat homemade Halloween treats. But Mrs. Sweet is certainly the last person you'd suspect of wanting to poison kids.

The man in the next apartment was giving Knievel a hard time.

"Blasted kids, always waking people up. Why don't you go play in the street?" He scratched the bald dome above his fringe of gray hair, then rubbed his eyes as he saw me. "Good grief, is that Bo Peep with a green face or am I drunk?"

He probably *was* drunk, judging by the way he rocked on his feet and clutched a glass I suspected wasn't ice water. He grinned at Susannah and me.

"Come in, come in, little ladies." He opened the door wide. "Uncle Bob's always got something nice for pretty girls. Even Bo Peeps with green faces."

Susannah shot me a look that said she was thinking what I was. "Thanks, but we'll just wait here."

He cocked his head and chuckled. "Now you're not afraid of Uncle Bob, are you?" He tried to pinch Susannah's chin, but she ducked. "Uncle

Bob wouldn't hurt you. And he's got lots of candy."

He stumbled back into the apartment, returning with chocolate mint patties wrapped in green tinfoil.

"Don't be shy, girls — take a couple. You can have one, too," he added grudgingly to Knievel. "One, I said," as Knievel grabbed a fistful and dashed off ahead of us. "Hey, girls!" Uncle Bob called after us. "Come back later."

"Let's hope he doesn't hold his breath till we do." Susannah grinned at me as we squeaked to a halt by the door Knievel was banging on. She glanced at her watch. "Hey, Grandpa's picking us up at your place in twenty minutes. Let's see if Carla's back and get going. You're riding with us, aren't you, Knievel?"

"Yeah. But there's still time to clean up here if these turkeys will open up." He gave the next door a whack, then kicked it. "Somebody's there. I heard them turn off the TV."

The door opened a crack and a very white face peered out.

"Go away!" gasped the pale little man.

3

He gawked at us with watery blue eyes, his buckteeth chattering and his nose twitching. He reminded me of a starved white rabbit. His name, printed on the door card, was O'Hare.

"Trick or treat," we repeated as he stared.

"Oh," Mr. O'Hare said at last. "Oh, you just wanted candy." He looked relieved. "Well, there's no candy here. Candy's bad for you. But of course, you wouldn't know that." He nodded knowingly. "The manufacturers keep it secret that sugar is poisonous."

I glanced at Susannah and we silently agreed we were wasting our time. But Knievel wouldn't take no for an answer.

"You must have something," he insisted, squirming through the door.

The rabbit looked alarmed. "Stay right there," he squeaked. "I'll get you something. Don't move."

I followed Knievel into the living room. Seeing

us, Mr. O'Hare slammed a door he'd just started to open down the hall.

"Stay there." Shaking a finger at us, he scurried back into the kitchen.

Knievel shrugged. "Some weirdo, huh?" He leaned against a hat rack by the door and helped himself to a beret hanging on it.

"Probably just into health foods. Looks like he's a vegetarian," said Susannah, eyeing a plate of carrots, brown rice, and brussels sprouts on the coffee table. She sniffed with a puzzled frown. "Funny a vegetarian would smoke."

"Sure reads lots of newspapers," I noted. There were stacks of them piled everywhere.

"But where's the TV?" Susannah looked around. "I'm sure I heard one before we came in."

Knievel tried on a huge fur hat that slid over his nose. "How do I look?"

"Not half bad," I said. "The half the hat covers, that is."

"I wonder why he wants a fur hat in California." Susannah took the hat and examined the label. "He doesn't seem the type who goes up to Tahoe to ski. Interesting. It's from a store in Illinois and looks brand-new."

Mr. O'Hare returned with a dusty jar full of sticky-looking green candies. "Lime honey delights from the natural food store," he said proudly. "Better for you than that machine-made poison they teach you to eat."

We each took one, thanked him, and skittered

out the door. He locked it behind us, and we heard him put up the chain.

"And after all that," I grumbled, "we can't eat his yucky old candy because it isn't even wrapped, much less sealed. That doesn't bother Knievel, though. Hey, come on. He's getting ahead of us."

Susannah nodded absently. "Curious that Mr. O'Hare eats in his living room with the TV on in his bedroom. Wonder why?" Count on her to play detective at a time like this.

"Why not? These apartments don't have dining rooms, for one thing. Anyway, who cares? Let's get going."

Catching up with Knievel, we collected lollipops, raisins, and packets of candy corn from the apartments across the hall, then raced upstairs.

Knievel was battering the nearest door with both fists when we arrived.

"Nobody's home, Knievel," said Susannah. "Can't you see that? Use your head."

"Wish you hadn't said that," I groaned, "Now he'll butt the door down."

But luckily a white-haired woman peeked out. "I *thought* I heard someone," she said triumphantly, offering us little Hershey bars out of a bag. "Next time don't knock so softly, my dears. I'm a bit hard of hearing."

I beat Knievel to the next door, where the people only had one lollipop left. Knievel thought I should give it to him, if you can believe it, because I had more than he did. Like it was my fault he got started late.

We collected bubble gum, Sugar Babies, Snickers, and other stuff along the hall. Then Susannah checked her watch and said we had to go.

"Once more," Knievel insisted, attacking the last door. As he knocked, I read the card taped to the door: D. D. MORDECAI.

"Trick or Tr-r-reee — " Knievel ended in a squeak as the door slowly screeched open.

There stood the tallest, thinnest man I've ever seen. But the ghastly thing was his eyes. They were completely white.

"Yes-s-s," he whispered. "You wish to view the deceased? Do come in."

The room was dark except for four tall candles flickering at the corners of a black box with a wreath on it.

I licked my lips. "Well, we, er — that is, we d-didn't know — so excuse us and we'll be go — "

The sightless skeleton gripped my arm. "Oh, but you mustn't leave yet. Jeremiah wouldn't like that. You must pay your respects."

And before I knew it, Mr. Mordecai pulled me through the door and right up to the black box. I turned to run, and there were Susannah and Knievel beside me.

Mr. Mordecai rubbed his hands and smiled shyly. "I'll be back," he whispered. And then he vanished. I mean it. One moment he was there, and the next he wasn't.

"Did you see that?" I gasped. But Susannah and Knievel were staring at the coffin.

"You suppose there's a real body in there?" Knievel whispered as somewhere mournful organ music began.

"Yes," Susannah said softly. "He wouldn't buy an expensive wreath like that for an empty coffin. But I wonder why the florist put *these* in the wreath? Unless — " Frowning thoughtfully, she fingered a stem of gray green leaves. A sprig broke off in her hand.

She seemed more interested in the wreath than in where Mr. Mordecai had disappeared to. Well, if she wasn't worried, I sure wouldn't let on I was. Susannah usually knows what she's doing. Still, I wasn't eager to spend the evening in this place.

"Maybe we ought to get going," I said, trying to sound cool. "Your grandpa's probably waiting for us and — " I turned toward the door and caught my breath.

There stood Mr. Mordecai. He'd appeared out of nowhere.

He carried something covered with a black cloth. "But I *can't* let you go, can I? Poor Jeremiah wouldn't like that, you know."

I glanced at the others. If we all rushed the door together, we just might make it. But Susannah, keeping her gaze on Mr. Mordecai's empty eye sockets, walked straight toward him. She reached out and laid something on the black cloth.

"I'll bring you some more of this to put on Jeremiah's grave next time I come. My grandmother grows it in her garden. But now we have to go."

Mr. Mordecai's blank eyeballs looked down at the grayish leaves. Slowly he nodded. "But first you must have one of these. Jeremiah would want you to."

He lifted the black cloth from the tray he held. "Popcorn balls," he announced. "Jeremiah did so love popcorn."

Knievel and I hesitated, but when Susannah took one of the popcorn balls wrapped in green cellophane and dropped another into Carla's bag, we snatched ours and made for the door.

I grabbed Susannah's arm, but she lingered. "Grandmother grows hers for tea, but I suppose Jeremiah didn't care for tea."

"Quite right, my dear. Jeremiah took his straight."

Personally I didn't care how Jeremiah took his. I just wanted to get out of there. I took the stairs like I was training for the Olympics, and Knievel almost beat me to the first landing.

There we met Carla dressed in a witch's costume that, besides being too tight, looked like it had lost a fight with a lawn mower. Every kid in town must have tried it on. No wonder her face looked meaner than the mask she was holding.

"You promised to wait for me," she stormed.

"You're late," I shouted back. "You expect us

to stand downstairs all night in a dark hall?"

"Didn't Nadine let you in? I told her — "

Luckily Susannah arrived at that moment. "Oh, there you are, Carla, just in time. Here's your treat bag. It has everything we got."

"Huh," sulked Knievel. "That's more than I got."

"Good grief, Knievel," said Susannah, "I thought only cows had two stomachs. Are you trying to make the *Guinness Book of World Records*?"

"I can see the headline in the *Oakland Tribune* now," I put in. "East Bay Boy Faces Champion Hog in Pig-Out Finals at the Coliseum."

Knievel glared at me. "I see an even better headline: Little Bo Peep Strangled With Her Own Crook."

"I see another headline, if we don't hurry up," said Susannah. "Grandfather Abandons Four Kids. Come on, let's get going."

Outside the fog oozing in from the San Francisco Bay was turning to rain. Knievel changed his mind about trick-or-treating on the way, and we all raced to my place. A few minutes later we were safe in Judge Higgins' car — if you call being stuck in the backseat with Knievel safe. I spent most of the ride defending my treat bag. Knievel kept trying to steal the lollipop he felt I'd cheated him out of and helping himself to whatever else he could snatch. Things were getting rough until Judge Higgins barked, "Simmer down back there."

After that Knievel left me alone, sulking in silence.

It was pouring when we reached Susannah's house. A car blocked the driveway, so the judge let us out at the sidewalk.

"Everybody out on the curb side," he ordered, "and don't step in the gutter."

I crawled over Knievel, who still sat hunched silently between Carla and me. Just for fun, I snatched his treat bag on my way out. That woke him up. He tumbled out of the car, grabbed my arm — the one holding my bag — and I let go of his bag to defend mine. Next thing I knew, both bags were in the gutter.

"Now look what you've done!" I yelled. On hands and knees I tried to catch my bag as it sailed toward the drain, followed by a fleet of candy bars, lollipops, chocolate mint patties, and a green popcorn ball.

Knievel didn't seem to care. He was staring into the rain with a dismal look on his face.

"I feel sick," he muttered, weaved on his feet, and threw up.

Serves him right, I thought, as the judge bundled him back into the car and drove him home. "That'll teach him to eat like a pig," I said to Susannah.

Well, how was I to know he'd been poisoned?

4

Police Inspector Smith knew all about crime, but not much about kids.

"I know it's hard for you children to think that anybody would want to hurt your little playmate," he said after breaking the news to us in the principal's office next morning.

"No," I said. I could think of plenty of kids who'd love to murder Knievel sometimes. "But he isn't going to die, is he?" I couldn't picture Knievel doing a thing like that.

"No, no — don't worry your pretty head. Your little friend will be back playing with you in no time."

Brother, I thought, this guy must think we're in kindergarten.

Susannah was frowning thoughtfully over her glasses. "What kind of poison was it, Inspector? A soporific, a barbiturate, or a hallucinogen?" Susannah believes detectives should know all about poisonous drugs. "Not cyanide or strychnine, I hope. No, of course not — how dumb of me — he wouldn't recover from that so easily," she added to herself. "Then what was it, Inspector?"

Inspector Smith stared at her, his jaw hanging. Nobody had told him about Susannah, I could see.

"Well, no," he wet his lips, "not cyanide or strychnine. Not a hallucinogen or barbiturate either. Actually, the hospital isn't sure *what* it was yet. We'll know soon, though." He flashed a smile that wasn't quite as confident as before.

"Thank you." Susannah pushed her glasses up again.

"Now girls," he went on in a serious voice, apparently deciding he could talk straight to us. "I want you to tell me everything that happened last night while you were with the Jones boy."

"Excuse me, Inspector" — Susannah looked worried — "there was another girl with us, Carla. At least she got the same treats Knievel did. And she's not at school today."

He frowned. "I know. The boy's mother gave me all your names. I called Carla's family before I talked to your folks a while ago. Carla's not feeling well — too much candy, her mother says. But she's taking her to the doctor to be on the safe side. Which reminds me" — he looked at me suspiciously — "your father says you dropped your candy in a gutter last night. Is that true?"

"You think I'm dumb enough to hide it to eat later?" I said huffily.

"Cool it, Lucy," Susannah murmured. "The inspector just wants the facts."

So I calmed down and gave him the story. "And if you don't believe me, ask Judge Higgins. He saw the whole thing."

"Okay, okay, I believe you." He scribbled in his note pad. "And that also accounts for the Jones boy's candy. Too bad."

"Sure is," sighed Susannah. "If we only had Knievel's bag, we'd know from what was left who *didn't* poison him. Well, mine's at home, and I didn't eat any of it — I couldn't, after all the ice cream and candy apples I ate at my party."

"Good," said Inspector Smith. "When the laboratory finishes analyzing it, we'll know which candy was poisoned."

"And that," Susannah sighed again, "will wrap up this case." I guessed she was a little sorry about that. Susannah was dying to find a new mystery to solve.

"Only if you got the same poisoned candy," said the inspector. "But — well, Lord knows where that kid had been before, and he's too sick to tell us right now."

"I'm pretty sure he got the poisoned candy when he was with us," Susannah said. "I don't think Knievel had done any trick-or-treating before he ran into us at the Eucalyptus Arms."

"That's right," I remembered. "He kept whining about it. Wonder what he was doing all afternoon?"

A cough came from the corner where the principal had sat quietly all this time. "I can answer that, Inspector. Knievel was right here in this office till past four-thirty. A little matter of the proper place to dispose of leftover pizza, which as I pointed out, was not under his neighbor just as he sat down."

The principal said he'd driven Knievel home just after four-thirty, had a talk with his mom, and last saw his favorite headache racing down the street as a vampire shortly before five-thirty.

"Poor Knievel," he sighed. "I must visit him in the hospital tomorrow and take him some flowers — and his homework." That's our principal, all heart.

"See?" Susannah looked triumphantly at the inspector. "Knievel met us at five-thirty, so he couldn't have stopped on the way. Besides, there's nothing much but stores between his place and the Eucalyptus Arms."

Inspector Smith shrugged. "Leave the detective work to the police, young lady. But you can help by telling us which people gave you what candy."

So we settled down and told him.

Afterwards, we got to ride in a patrol car to the Eucalyptus Arms. I couldn't help feeling guilty that Knievel was missing all the excitement. Gross as he was, things were going to be dull without him. Well, the hospital wouldn't put up with him any longer than they had to, so he'd probably be home soon.

Inspector Smith left us in the car with a patrolman while he went in to see the manager. He returned scowling.

"Carla's in the hospital. Same symptoms the Jones kid had."

"What symptoms?" Susannah asked.

Without answering, he opened the rear door for us. "Okay, kids, come with me."

I thought he was taking us to identify the suspects, but no such luck. All we did was go down to the manager's apartment, where Carla's stepfather, Mr. Able, showed us a plan of the building. Each of the twelve apartments had the name of the tenant written on it.

"I made this copy for you," Mr. Able said to Inspector Smith. "You can cross off those two apartments because that one's vacant and the folks in the other one were out of town."

The inspector has us point to each apartment and tell what we'd gotten there. Some, like the apartments labeled Sweet, O'Hare, and Mordecai, were easy to remember, but others weren't. The inspector checked what we said against the list he'd made in the principal's office, and made notes. We ended up sure of six apartments, pretty sure of one, disagreed on one, and couldn't remember what the other two had given us.

"It doesn't matter," Susannah shrugged.

"Whatever they gave us was the kind of stuff you buy in plastic bags at the grocery store. The poison must have been in something that was homemade — or anyway, unwrapped."

Inspector Smith grunted as if she'd read his mind and he didn't much like it. "You got some unwrapped things, didn't you?" He flipped back through his note pad.

"Sure," I said, "but we know not to eat it." Remembering Mrs. Sweet's cupcakes, I added, "Unless we know the person is okay. I just took that rabbit's junk to be polite."

"Mr. O'Hare, she means," Susannah explained to the inspector, who looked up puzzled.

"But I suppose the Jones boy wasn't as fussy as you two about what he ate?"

"Well, he did seem to feel a bit — uh, undernourished," Susannah agreed. "I noticed he was eating everything as fast as he got it. I think we can be reasonably sure he ate all the suspicious stuff."

The inspector, I could see, was beginning to discover that Susannah usually knew what she was talking about. He nodded, scribbled on his note pad, folded up the map of the building, and motioned us out the door.

"Hope you catch that rat soon," growled Mr. Able as we were leaving. "What kind of maniac would poison poor little Carla? 'Course, I've got my share of weirdos here. O'Hare for one, and

Mordecai's pretty balmy, if you ask me. That guy gives me the creeps, for all his smiling and fine manners."

"Yeah?" Inspector Smith got out his note pad again. "What's so strange about those two?"

"Nothing I can put my finger on," Mr. Able admitted. "But for one thing, neither of them ever seems to have a visitor. A couple of hermits, both of them. Bob says even Mrs. Sweet can't make friends with Mordecai. He — "

"Bob who?" Inspector Smith interrupted.

"Bob Jensen in 1-C, the one the kids call Uncle Bob. By the way, you can forget about Bob. I've known him for years, ever since we worked together in Los Angeles. He used to baby-sit Nadine when she was little. Matter of fact, Bob got me the job here when the last manager left this summer. Now about Mordecai," Mr. Able added, "there *is* one funny thing. Somebody named Fluggenheimer signs his rent checks."

"Interesting," Susannah muttered, glancing at me.

Inspector Smith gave her a sharp look and snapped his note pad shut. "After I take these kids home, I want you to tell me about Mordecai and all your other tenants. And I want to talk to them myself and pick up their leftover candy."

So back to the patrol car we went and on to Susannah's. Pop was letting me spend the night with her, as I often did on Fridays, even though this time her grandparents were away. After meeting her Aunt Louise, who was staying with us, Pop had grinned and said he thought she could handle me.

"When are you going to arrest somebody?" I asked the inspector as we rode along.

"As soon as I've got some solid evidence," said Inspector Smith. "And that, Susannah, is what your trick-or-treat bag will give us."

Susannah frowned thoughtfully over her glasses. "I hope you're right, Inspector."

5

"Interesting," Susannah muttered a half hour later, as we sprawled in front of her TV. Inspector Smith had dropped us off just in time to catch the end of a soccer game.

"Interesting? This game?" I glared at the screen. "Even Knievel's a better forward than *that* turkey."

"I meant this." Turning down the sound, Susannah handed me the paper she'd been scribbling on. "So far as I can see, the poisoner had to be one of these four people."

This was her list:

SWEET (Apartment 1-A) — Cupcakes
JENSEN (Uncle Bob) (Apartment 1-C) — Chocolate mint patties
O'HARE (Apartment 1-E) — Lime honey delights
MORDECAI (Apartment 2-B) — Popcorn balls

"Come on," I scoffed. "Mrs. Sweet? She's been giving kids cookies and candy for ages, and I never heard of anybody even getting a stomachache."

"I'm just considering the facts," Susannah said. "Those are the only people who gave us stuff that wasn't sealed."

"And what about Uncle Bob? You buy that kind of chocolate mint in a sealed box."

"True, but we didn't see him open the box. And it would be easy to pull back the foil from those patties, slip something under the chocolate coating, and wrap them back up. Who'd ever notice a little rough spot in the chocolate?"

"Not Knievel," I agreed. "And I wouldn't put it past old Uncle Bob to poison him. He sure didn't like Knievel."

"But why poison the rest of us? Whoever did this couldn't have known *who'd* get the poison. Funny thing," she frowned thoughtfully, "none of the little kids who came earlier got poisoned."

I considered that fact. "Maybe the poisoner wasn't home then, or just didn't answer the door. Hey, that's right." I sat up. "Remember, Uncle Bob was mad with Knievel for waking him up. He must have slept right through the other kids. And that weird rabbit guy, O'Hare — Knievel practically kicked down his door to get him to open up."

Susannah nodded. "And I got the impression we were Mr. Mordecai's first trick-or-treaters, too. But of course, Mrs. Sweet had plenty before us."

"Which proves she's innocent," I said, "or else every little kid around here would be in the hospital."

"Not necessarily. She might just have it in for older kids. Okay, okay, I agree she's not our prime suspect." Brushing away my argument, Susannah squinted over her glasses as if she'd just thought of something. "You know, the poisoner had to dispose of the evidence. I wonder if — " She glanced at her watch and jumped up. "There's just time to call and check before they close."

"Before who closes?" I asked as she raced to the phone. But then the doorbell started ringing and I had to run to the front door.

It was Susannah's Aunt Louise, still in her nurse's uniform. "Forgot my key. How are you, girl? And where's that niece of mine?"

Susannah, looking pleased about something, bounced into the hall to hug her.

"Did the police take that bag of candy your grandmother left for them on the hall table?" Aunt Louise demanded. When we said they had, she squeezed us again and rumpled our hair.

"Thank God you two didn't get poisoned by that maniac. When I think of that little Carla they brought in today vomiting and half out of her mind — but don't worry, she's all right now." Aunt Louise nursed at Children's Hospital. "Well, come on, you lazy brats," she added gruffly, pushing us toward the kitchen. "Help me make dinner."

As Susannah and I sliced carrots together, I whispered, "Who were you calling just now?"

"The Sanitation Department, of course," Susannah whispered back. "And sure enough, they said the Eucalyptus Arms has the same schedule your place does. Aunt Louise," she added out loud, "do they know at the hospital what the poison was?"

"Not exactly." Aunt Louise closed the oven door and turned down the heat. "But it's a safe bet it wasn't really a poison, technically speaking."

"Not arsenic or cyanide or — ?"

"No way," Aunt Louise snorted, "or else those babies would be bye-bye by now."

"How about marijuana or LSD?"

"You kidding? That's the first thing they checked for — all the known hallucinogens, especially with that Jones boy babbling away about leading an army to attack Mars."

"Knievel would." I grinned.

Susannah carefully peeled a cucumber. "But if it wasn't poison or a hallucinogen, what was it?"

"Probably an overdose of some kind of strong medicine," said Aunt Louise, keeping one eye on the oven.

"A medicine?" I hadn't thought of that possibility.

"Sure. Any medicine strong enough to fight

whatever's attacking your body packs a real whammy. Believe me, medicine is nothing to play around with."

"If it *was* a medicine," said Susannah, "will the lab be able to figure out what it was?"

"Depends." Aunt Louise shrugged. "If it's something unusual, they may have trouble."

After supper Aunt Louise wanted to watch some sickening movie. I tried to tell her *The Revenge of the Vampire* on Channel 2 was better, but I wasted my breath. Anyway, she said, it was time we did our homework.

"Quit complaining." Susannah grinned as we went upstairs. "You've already seen *The Revenge of the Vampire* twice anyway."

"Three times," I corrected. "That's how I know it's so good. You ought to see Morton DeKay as the vampire. They don't make vampires like him anymore. Besides, who does homework on Friday night?"

Susannah dived onto her bed. "We might as well. What else have we got to do?"

She handed me my math book, and for three whole minutes I tried to figure out how long it would take a car going fifty-five miles an hour to go 846 miles.

"Well, what do you think?" Susannah looked up from her book, chin in hand.

"I think that anybody driving 846 miles at fifty-five miles an hour would have to stop to go to the bathroom now and then," I said, tossing my book toward her desk. "So how can I solve a dumb problem like that?"

"I meant, what do you think about this case, you twit."

"Well, one thing's for sure. Whatever flattened Knievel," I said, "was something green."

"Green? I hadn't thought of that. You're right, everything on my list *was* green. Mr. O'Hare's lime things, the icing on Mrs. Sweet's cupcakes — even the cellophane on the popcorn balls and the foil on the mint patties were green."

"It figures," I said, "coming from a building painted poison green."

"But I doubt that's going to help us solve this case," Susannah said.

"I hate to mention it, Sherlock, but the police don't need us to solve this case. By tomorrow they'll know exactly which thing in your bag had the poison — the medicine, I mean. Cheer up, though, we may get to testify in court."

"Terrific," Susannah said glumly. "But I suppose you're right. Too bad, Lucy. It could have been an interesting case."

She spoke too soon. Early next morning Inspector Smith phoned Susannah. Was she sure she'd given him *all* her Halloween treats? Was there anything, any little thing, she'd kept?

"No, everything was in that bag. You mean the lab didn't find the poison?"

* * *

After we'd cleaned up from breakfast, Susannah sat frowning over her glasses.

"Are we going to hang around here all day?" I demanded. "Why don't we go skate in the park or — "

"I've got a better idea. Let's go play some ball."

"Huh?" The idea of Susannah Higgins wanting to play softball boggled my mind. "You mean in the park?"

"Not exactly. I was thinking of some place quieter. Say, maybe that courtyard behind the Eucalyptus Arms."

I grinned. "Susannah, what kind of dirty business are you up to?"

"Dirty?" Susannah examined her fingernails. "Yes, you might say this is a dirty assignment, all right. You might say, in fact, that we're going to dig right to the bottom till we get to the rotten truth."

"Yeah? And just where are we going to be digging for this rotten truth?"

"In the garbage cans, my dear fellow detective."

6

So shortly after nine o'clock we strolled down the driveway of the Eucalyptus Arms into the paved yard behind. I was tossing my softball so anybody could see we were just two kids fooling around on a Saturday morning.

And, as a matter of fact, I had a feeling somebody was watching. Glancing up, I saw a curtain move in a first-floor window — O'Hare's, I thought.

The garbage cans were lined up against the far side of the carport, out of sight from the back windows and the driveway.

"How are we ever going to find one little medicine bottle in a whole can of garbage?" I asked.

"The cans shouldn't be very full because they were emptied two days ago." Susannah kept her voice low. "I remembered they picked up your garbage Halloween with your costume in it and figured this block might have the same schedule. I checked with the Sanitation Department, and sure enough."

"So everything in these cans got put there since Halloween morning."

"Right." Susannah handed me one of her grandmother's pink and yellow gardening gloves and drew the other on her hand. "You take the cans marked 1-A and 1-C — that's Mrs. Sweet's and Uncle Bob's apartments, according to Mr. Able's building plan. I'll take O'Hare's and Mordecai's."

"Careful," she warned as I lifted a lid. "Look out for glass and stuff like drain cleaner that could burn through these gloves. See any bottles in Uncle Bob's can?"

"Lots," I said. "Beer bottles, gin bottles, vodka — take your pick." I lifted them out one by one, but there was no little medicine bottle underneath. Sighing, I emptied two sacks onto one of the newspapers we'd brought. I poked daintily through the coffee grounds, grapefruit hulls, steak bones, and TV dinner cartons. There were also a couple of magazines with dirty pictures in them. Shaking my head at Susannah, I poured the whole mess back into the sacks, then shoved everything back into Uncle Bob's garbage can.

I paused to peer over Susannah's shoulder as she sifted through the single bag in Mr. Mordecai's can. The contents surprised me because they were so ordinary. Orange peelings, soggy tea bags, Chinese takeout cartons, a nearly full can of cat food, soup cans, TV dinner boxes, and two empty containers labeled Hot Buttered Popcorn.

Susannah sat on her haunches fingering a scrap

of white net fabric with two small ovals cut out of it. "Interesting," she muttered. She poked a dried blob of catsup and picked up a small flattened tube, which she cleaned on her jeans.

"Surgical glue. Hmm." She shoved the tube and the fabric into her pocket, then dumped the rest of the stuff back into the sack. "Come on, we've got to hurry before somebody finds us here."

Mrs. Sweet's can held a neatly tied plastic bag. Inside was a flour sack, a milk carton, walnut shells, an empty bag for chocolate chips, and all the jars, bottles, peelings, and eggshells you'd expect a good cook to throw out. But no little medicine bottle.

"Strange." Susannah was peering into the 1-E can. "Mr. O'Hare sure eats a lot for such a skinny man." The can held two full sacks of garbage. The first one overflowed with withered carrots, honey jars, oatmeal boxes, Hershey bar wrappers, a steak bone, and yogurt cartons. Susannah had just taken out the second bag when we heard heavy footsteps in the driveway.

"Emergency plan!" Susannah gasped.

I shoved the plastic bag back into Mrs. Sweet's can and turned to help Susannah. As I snatched up one of her bags, it sprang a leak. Coffee grounds, rotten squash, and oatmeal spewed over my jeans.

As I crammed the dripping bag into the can, the footsteps stalked across the yard and past the carport, then stopped.

"What are you kids up to?" demanded a gruff voice. Jerking around, I saw two tough-looking men in leather jackets.

"Who, us?" I tried to look like an innocent kid who just happened to be resting against an open garbage can.

"We're looking for our ball," Susannah said, sidling up beside me and reaching into my back pocket. "I thought I saw it land somewhere right around — oh, there it is," she exclaimed, turning around and snatching it out of O'Hare's garbage can. Which didn't surprise me, since she'd just slipped it out of my pocket and dropped it there.

"All right now, let's play some ball here!" Susannah sprinted far left and hurled a wild one that shaved one man's cheek. "Oops, sorry." Susannah is not destined for Baseball's Hall of Fame.

"Do California a favor, kid," said the man, after checking to be sure he still had his mustache. "Go East for your baseball career. That's a funny mitt you've got there," he added, staring suspiciously at my flowered gardening glove.

"Yeah, I know." I sniffed. "Everybody makes fun of it. I'm saving up my lunch money for a real one." I leaped for a high one before it could crash through a window. Playing catch with Susannah is great fielding practice.

"Well, suppose you kids go play somewhere else for awhile," growled the man.

"Oh, we can't leave the yard." I nodded toward the building as if we lived there. I guessed the men wouldn't know the difference. They probably weren't tenants either, since they'd walked around from the street.

The men shrugged and walked over to the garbage cans. There they put on leather gloves and started going through the garbage cans, tossing stuff into plastic bags. We played catch and pretended not to notice. That was hard to do, especially when the bossy one hauled out the rotting bag we'd just shoved back into O'Hare's can. He cursed as coffee grounds and oatmeal slopped over his trousers. "Watch your language," the other man snapped. "The kids can hear."

We sure were *trying* to hear, but the men didn't say much. We couldn't tell if they found anything either. Finally, they shoved the last bag back. They barely glanced at us as they walked back up the driveway to the street.

I waited until I couldn't hear their footsteps.

"Plainclothes cops?" I asked Susannah.

She nodded. "I *thought* Inspector Smith would think of the garbage cans. Good thing we got here first. Oh, good morning, Mr. Able," she added loudly. "How's Carla?"

The manager was coming up the basement steps with Nadine behind him.

"Much better, thanks. The doctor thinks we can bring her home tomorrow. We're just going to meet her mother at the hospital."

"Poor dear little Carla," Nadine said sourly. "How she must be suffering, with everybody bringing her presents and making a fuss over her. She's going to hate having to come home."

"Nadine," Mr. Able said sharply, "you promised to be nice to Carla today."

"Okay, okay. I suppose she really *is* sick. Maybe now she knows how that feels. I'll behave myself at the hospital, if you swear you'll get me to cheerleading practice on time."

"I said I would, didn't I?"

Mr. Able was starting for the carport when Susannah asked, "Mr. Able, how long has Mr. Mordecai lived here?"

Mr. Able blinked, surprised. "Six months about. Why?"

"Well, Lucy and I were thinking we might earn some money doing errands for your tenants. Bringing up their groceries, walking their dogs — that kind of thing. But we want to make sure they're okay people first. So would you tell us a few things about them. Take Mrs. Sweet — "

"A very nice lady," Mr. Able said sternly. "Now look, you kids think of some other way to earn money. Go home, hear me? Go home. Somebody in this building wants to kill kids."

There was nothing we could do but leave.

"Blast," muttered Susannah as we walked back up the driveway. "People never want to tell kids the facts. I'm afraid we're going to have to dig harder for them, Lucy."

She wasn't kidding.

7

Knievel looked awful. Even worse than usual, I mean. Propped up in bed at Children's Hospital, he was busily shredding a worn edge of the sheet. Clearly, Knievel was dying a slow, cruel death of incurable boredom.

"Cheer up," I said. "Things could be worse. The coach put Roger in your position on the soccer team. So don't worry, between the two of us we'll beat Jefferson next week without you."

Luckily he had nothing heavier than a pillow to hurl. From the way he threw it, I judged Knievel was about to make a fast recovery.

Two old friends were keeping him company, Juliet Travis and her mother. I hadn't seen them since they'd moved to San Francisco. Juliet's right cheek was bandaged.

"What happened?" I began before realizing, "Oh, you had your operation."

Juliet touched the bandage. "Just wait till this comes off. The doctor says you won't be able to tell where the burn scar was."

"Thanks to you, Susannah," Mrs. Travis said warmly, "and you, too, Lucy and Knievel, for solving our mystery. When Juliet's bandages come off, we're celebrating with a big party in your honor."

"Maybe a *little* party would be nicer," said Juliet, who hated crowds. "Susannah, have you figured out who poisoned Knievel yet?"

"Not yet," Susannah admitted. "There are some puzzling angles to this case."

"Juliet sweetie" — Mrs. Travis smiled as she got up to leave — "we both know Susannah is a great detective, but this is a case for the police."

"I bet Susannah will solve it," Juliet said stubbornly as they left.

"I wish I were so sure of that," Susannah sighed as the door closed. "Right now, we don't have much to go on — unless you've got some idea, Knievel, how you got poisoned."

"Sure. Like I told the cops, it was something I ate in the car. Yuck, was it gross — I could puke just thinking about that taste. I felt fine before that. But," he sighed, "I can't remember what is was."

"Some detective you are." Susannah propped her chin in her hand. "Then what did it taste like? Bitter? Sour?"

"Sort of salty, but sweet — sickening sweet. Only it was worse, like medicine. I can't describe it."

"Tastes are hard to describe," Susannah

agreed. "But try to think what it was. Mrs. Sweet's cupcakes?"

"No, they were great, and anyway I ate them long before we got to the car."

"How about those chocolate mints Uncle Bob gave us? Or those green things from Mr. O'Hare? Or — "

Knievel shook his head. "I can't remember."

"But he ate all that stuff before he got in the car," I pointed out. "In fact, he shoveled everything into his mouth as fast as he got it."

"True," said Susannah. "But he also helped himself to your loot in the backseat. Could be it was a second helping of something that did him in. Remember what you took out of Lucy's bag, Knievel?"

Knievel didn't. In fact, the whole subject seemed to make him nauseated. He muttered something about never touching the stuff again. From now on, it was strictly meat and vegetables for him. Which was a good thing, for his lunch of spinach and chicken arrived just then, along with his mother and my father.

Seeing our parents together never does much for my mood, or Knievel's either for that matter. The one thing Knievel and I have in common is a burning ambition never to end up brother and sister. Single parents, let me tell you, can be a problem. Susannah didn't have to urge me to leave and go with her to visit Carla.

Upstairs in Carla's ward, her family was just leaving.

"We must go now, darling," her mother said anxiously. "Nadine has to get to cheerleader practice, and then we have to buy groceries. Anyway, now you have some friends here to keep you company."

Carla turned away as her mother tried to kiss her.

"Oh, brother," Nadine muttered, "that brat deserves an Oscar for her 'poor me' act."

"Nadine!" Mr. Able snapped, going to pat Carla's shoulder. "Carla honey, we'll be here to take you home first thing tomorrow. You'll be all right with your friends here, and then you can watch TV."

"Yeah, enjoy yourself, kid," Nadine said nastily. "Maybe now *you'll* learn what fun it is being sick."

Carla turned to stick out her tongue at Nadine. "That witch," she snarled as the door closed behind them. "Why did they have to bring her?"

"Well, she *is* your sister," I pointed out.

Carla shot up from her pillows. "Nadine is *not* my sister. She's just the daughter of my stepfather. I never even saw her till after Mom married him last year. They let Nadine come live with us just before we moved to the Eucalyptus Arms because she was supposed to be sick. And boy, can she work a sick act! There Nadine was lazing in bed, polishing her nails and watching TV, while

Mom fixed special meals for her and I brought them to her on a tray. It's killing her" — she grinned — "that I have to stay in bed when I come home and she'll have to bring *me* trays."

"Seems fair," Susannah agreed, and quickly changed the subject. "Do you know what it was that made you sick?"

Carla's grin faded. "No," she said, her mouth tight. "And I'm sick of talking about it. The police, my folks — everybody's been asking me. All I know is I ate some stuff in that bag and got sick. I don't remember anything else."

"Sure," Susannah nodded understandingly. "Only, what did you do with your trick-or-treat bag?"

"I told you, I can't remember. I tried, but it's no use."

"Oh, well, maybe the police will find it. Remember what you ate out of it?"

"No." Carla sighed heavily. "Look, I don't want to talk about it."

I was getting annoyed. "Carla, if you don't cooperate, how can we track down the poisoner? You want him to get away with this?"

"Of course not," Carla snapped. "But what makes you think you two can do any better than the police?"

"Maybe we can't," Susannah said, "but it won't hurt to try. Remember if anything you ate before you got sick tasted — well, funny?"

Carla lay back on her pillows, reflecting. "Something did taste kind of bitter, but I can't remember what it was."

"Uh-huh." Susannah scribbled in her notebook. "Interesting. Now tell us something about the people who live in your building. Let's start with Mrs. Sweet."

Carla jerked up from her pillows. "Don't you dare accuse Mrs. Sweet of poisoning me. She's the nicest person in the whole building — in this whole city, for that matter. She always has time to talk when I go see her. And she listens to me — I mean, really listens. Never tells me I'm wrong and Nadine is right, like my mother does. She just lets me talk. And she knows how I feel. She says I remind her of her daughter who died," Carla added almost shyly. "So don't you pick on Mrs. Sweet."

"Sorry, I was just asking." Susannah looked up from her note pad. "What about Mr. Mordecai?"

"You mean that weird man who always wears dark glasses?" Carla shivered. "He gives me shivers. Nobody knows anything about him, not even Mrs. Sweet."

"What about Uncle Bob?"

Carla fidgeted with her blanket. "What do you want to know? Ask my stepfather. He and Uncle Bob are old friends. That's how come Uncle Bob got my stepfather the job managing the Eucalyptus Arms."

"You must see a lot of Uncle Bob then."

Carla shrugged. "He's always wanting to take me to the movies and the zoo and places. Mom doesn't understand why I won't go."

Susannah gave her a keen look over her glasses. "Maybe she thinks you're just being rude to your stepfather's friend."

Carla nodded. "That's it. Even Mrs. Sweet thinks Uncle Bob is a nice man."

"Hmm." Susannah picked up her pencil again. "Now what about Mr. O'Hare?"

"Who? Oh, that skinny, nervous man who acts like he's afraid of his shadow? Well, I know one thing." Carla's eyes danced. "He must have a girl friend somewhere who writes to him."

"What makes you think that?"

"Because once when we were both getting the mail out of our boxes, he dropped a letter as he was going back inside. When I ran after him and gave it to him, he nearly had a fit. Like he thought I might have opened it. He's strange, that guy."

"Interesting." Susannah put away her notebook as Carla's chicken and spinach arrived. "We better go get some lunch, too. See you when you get back home."

We walked back to the bus stop. Pop had offered us a ride, but I'd preferred to hit him up for the bus fare instead.

"A fat lot of help Knievel and Carla were," I griped. "You'd think they'd remember what it was that tasted so awful."

"Strange," said Susannah. "Carla thought it was bitter, and Knievel said it was salty and sweet."

I tried to imagine a taste like that. Maybe lemons, potato chips, and molasses all mushed together. "Yuck. They must be nuts to eat something like that."

"Exactly," said Susannah, as we got on the bus. "Now if we can only figure out what it was."

At the stop just before mine, she suddenly decided to get off.

"See that natural foods store on the corner? Bet it's the one Mr. O'Hare shops at. Want to try that green candy he gave us?"

It was lunchtime and I hadn't had anything but bubble gum in my mouth since breakfast, so I was ready for almost anything. But lime honey delights?

"You want to find out if they taste funny?"

"Well, anyway, if they're salty or bitter. Relax." Susannah grinned. "You won't get poisoned in a health food store."

Maybe not. But the jars of dried seaweed and pineapple, and the open bins of brown rice and sprouted wheat didn't look like anything I'd ever seen in a grocery store. I wrinkled my nose. "What kind of nuts eat this junk?"

Susannah looked amused. "Aunt Louise, for one. Didn't I tell you she's a vegetarian? And from the way you snarfed down her supper last night,

I think I know another natural foods junkie."

As we turned into the next aisle, where a man stood filling a bag with almonds, Susannah grabbed my arm.

"Oh look, Lucy," she said loudly. "There's the cashew-date butter Aunt Louise turned us on to last night. Let's get some. Excuse me, sir." Susannah reached over the man's head for the jar on the top shelf, but couldn't quite make it.

"Here, let me." Mr. O'Hare set down his almonds beside his newspapers and fetched down the jar. "I'm glad to see some children know what real food is."

Smiling, he turned to hand Susannah the jar, but she was looking down at his newspaper. Abruptly he thrust the jar at me, his smile gone. Snatching up his newspapers and almonds, he dashed off.

"Think he recognized us from Halloween?" I whispered as we headed for the checkout counter.

"I doubt it. Halloween costumes make great disguises." Susannah reached into the jar of green candies on the counter and took out four. "How much money have you got on you?"

We scraped our pockets, paid the cashier, then headed uphill munching our lime honey delights.

"Well, what do you think?" Susannah chewed thoughtfully as we walked. "Doesn't taste salty or bitter to me."

"Me either. Just tastes like lime gumdrops. Not

bad, in fact, and I usually don't like gumdrops. Of course, it would be easy to slip something into stuff this soft."

"True," said Susannah, "but it would be just as easy to slip something into the cupcakes, the chocolate mints, or the popcorn balls. The question is, what tasted so ghastly that Knievel and Carla forgot the taste of the candy it was in?"

"That's a good point," I reflected. "They didn't remember tasting chocolate, lime, popcorn, or mint."

We walked awhile in silence. "You know," I remarked, "Mr. O'Hare seemed kind of nice today, getting down that jar for us. Not like Halloween when he acted so — " I tried to think of the word.

"Scared? That's how he seemed to me, Lucy — scared." Susannah nibbled at her green candy. "Now why was he so scared on Halloween? And why did he get so scared today when he saw me looking at his Chicago newspaper?"

8

As we passed the Eucalyptus Arms, Susannah stopped.

"Let's give Mrs. Sweet a visit. She knows more than anybody about the people in this building. Anyway, I could do with a cookie or two."

I wasn't about to argue. This was my idea of detective work.

While we were ringing Mrs. Sweet's bell, the mail carrier swung up the steps and began stuffing the mail boxes. Susannah straightened her glasses to watch.

"Mr. O'Hare sure gets a lot of letters," she commented.

"Really. Even more than usual today," said the mail carrier. "Funny, he never used to get anything but bills up till a few weeks ago. Must have joined a lonely hearts club or something." He reached past us to press a bell. "He likes me to let him know when his mail's here." Shouldering his bag, he moved on to the next building.

Mrs. Sweet didn't answer her bell. We were

heading back to the sidewalk when, through the fronds of the palm tree, we saw Mr. O'Hare scurrying down the street with a load of bags and newspapers.

"Time to disappear," Susannah whispered, nudging me around the building into the driveway. "He'll get paranoid if we're here right after he just saw us in the store."

"Para — what? You mean he'll think we're spying on him?" I've gotten pretty good at translating Susannah into English. "Well, we are, aren't we?"

I peered around the building to watch him unload his mailbox. He glanced at each envelope before unlocking the front door and diving inside.

"What did you say?" I asked as Susannah dragged me back. I couldn't hear her over the TV blasting from the window above.

"I said it's interesting he leaves his TV on when he goes out," she repeated louder. "Makes you wonder if — "

"What on earth are you girls doing there?"

Mrs. Sweet stared at us from the entrance to the driveway, her arms full of grocery bags. "If you've come to see Carla, she won't be home till tomorrow. I'm going to visit her at the hospital this evening, poor dear."

"Too bad we missed her." Susannah's glance warned me to let Mrs. Sweet think we *had* come to see Carla. It was simpler than trying to explain why we were hiding in the driveway.

"Poor Carla's had a rough time of it," Mrs. Sweet said as we hauled her grocery bags upstairs. "First having to move away from her old friends, then getting used to a new stepfather and stepsister. Now this," she sighed as she opened her door. "Just set those bags anywhere. How about some brownies?"

We said we just might manage one or two.

"I heard that the police think somebody in this building poisoned Carla," Susannah remarked before Mrs. Sweet could change the subject.

"So they said." Mrs. Sweet's smile was grim. "I got the feeling they consider me a prime suspect."

"That's silly," I burst out. "If you wanted to poison kids, you could have done it thousands of times."

"Thanks, dear. Just call me the Rotten Tooth Fairy. I sometimes think Jim O'Hare is right that I'd do you all a favor by passing out sunflower seeds instead of cookies and candy."

"Mr. O'Hare's a vegetarian, isn't he?" Susannah asked casually.

"That's right. Never touches meat."

"No wonder he's so scrawny and pale," I said.

"Oh, most vegetarians are quite healthy," Mrs. Sweet said. "I think Jim O'Hare has some condition that makes him look so unwell."

"What kind of condition?" Susannah's eyes lit up. I could see she was dying to find out if he took medicine.

"I've no idea. Actually, I don't really know him all that well. He used to drop in for a cup of tea now and then, but lately he hardly even speaks to me in the hall. I wonder if I said something to offend him."

"Maybe he's just busy," I suggested.

"I doubt it. He never goes anywhere, and I've never seen anybody come visit him."

"Doesn't he go to work?" I asked.

"He's retired. I believe his parents died and left him some money before he moved here from Illinois a couple of years ago."

"Hasn't he got any family or friends?" asked Susannah.

Mrs. Sweet shook her head. "He's mentioned a half brother back in Chicago, but I gather they're not on good terms. No, Jim's a loner. Seems to do nothing but sit home watching TV lately. Funny, I thought he hated TV. Bob, who lives next to him, is always complaining about the noise."

"Uncle Bob, you mean?"

Mrs. Sweet smiled. "I thought only Carla and Nadine called him that. Poor Bob, I was so worried about him when he heard Carla had been poisoned. He has a bad heart and it's not good for him to get upset."

I glanced at Susannah. That made two suspects who might take some kind of medicine.

"Do you know Mr. Mordecai?" I asked.

Mrs. Sweet rubbed her forehead as if she hardly heard me. "Who? Oh, that strange man upstairs. He bows to me when we pass, but never stops to chat. Nobody seems to know him. He's kept to himself ever since he moved here last spring. From Los Angeles, I believe. Always seems to wear dark glasses, even indoors."

"Do you know if he does much cooking?" Susannah asked.

I wondered why she wanted to know that.

Mrs. Sweet shook her head. "I wouldn't know. Look, girls, you'll have to excuse me now. I'm getting a headache. I get them a lot this time of year. All I can do is take my medicine and go to bed."

"I'm sorry," Susannah said. "Are you allergic to something?"

"So the doctor says. But I think it may have something to do with losing my little girl about this time a few years ago." She pressed her lips together in a sad smile as she opened the door. "She'd be just about your age now."

"You mean your allergy is psychosomatic?" Susannah asked.

"Exactly. But the pills help. At least, they knock me out for a few hours."

I waited until we were outside. "*Psychosomatic*, huh?" I poked Susannah in the ribs. "Dare you to spell it. Don't tell me — it means your illness is all in your mind, doesn't it?"

"Something like that. But psychosomatic or not, it's interesting that Mrs. Sweet takes strong medicine for her headaches."

The fog was moving in. Beyond the next corner everything faded away into gray nothingness as if the world ended there. Fog gives me the eerie feeling that something I can't see is going to pounce out at me. That's why I started when a long, thin figure appeared from nowhere in the next block.

Susannah saw him, too, and caught my arm. I fought the impulse to run as the man, without waiting for the green light, started across the street. Brakes screeched and a driver shouted. He kept coming toward us, his dark glasses staring straight ahead.

"Mr. Mordecai," Susannah spoke softly.

The dark glasses turned toward her. "Yes-s?"

"Did you bury Jeremiah?"

A silence. "Yes-s. I've just come from the cemetery."

"Oh," said Susannah, and after a pause. "Well, good-bye, Mr. Mordecai."

Bowing to us, he walked on into the fog behind us.

I dragged Susannah across the street. "That guy's weird," I gasped as we reached the corner. "He's not for real."

"Exactly," said Susannah. She gazed thoughtfully over her glasses. "Odd that nobody seems to know anything about Mr. Mordecai."

I was almost sure I heard footsteps behind us. Snatching Susannah's hand, I ran her the next two blocks. She was winded by the time we reached my building. I looked around and listened as I got out my key.

A shadow leaped out of the darkness.

"You dumb cat!" I exploded. "Skat! Go back where you belong and quit bothering us."

Susannah scooped up the little black blob. "Poor thing's hungry, Lucy."

"I can't help that. We've got a cat already, and that's one more than we're supposed to have. If the landlord finds out about Puffin — well, if you're so worried about it, be my guest and take him home."

"Grandpa's allergic to cats." She hugged the kitten regretfully. "Well, come on, you. I'll find you a home somewhere." She carried the cat inside while I turned on the TV and went to find something to eat. It was long past lunchtime, and Mrs. Sweet's brownies felt pretty lonesome in my stomach. Pop had left a baked chicken in the refrigerator.

"Interesting," Susannah remarked as I set out the chicken, some apples, bread, and milk. "Mrs. Sweet had a daughter who'd be our age now." She shredded a drumstick and put it on a paper napkin for the kitten.

"Are you saying Mrs. Sweet tried to poison us just because her daughter's dead and we're alive? That's crazy."

"True. But anybody who poisons kids has a crazy reason, Lucy. And it's odd none of the younger kids who came earlier got poisoned."

"Look, if Mrs. Sweet wanted to, she could have poisoned us lots of times before." Somehow that thought reminded me uneasily of the brownies reposing under my belt. I hoped that rumble in my stomach was just hunger.

"But she couldn't get away with it like she could on Halloween. With everybody handing out goodies, who'd ever suspect her?"

"Not me," I said firmly as I tuned the TV. One of my favorite old horror movies was on. "It's a lousy thing if you can't trust your candy connection. Why pick on her when we've got Mordecai, O'Hare, and Uncle Bob to choose from?"

"They're certainly more likely suspects," Susannah agreed. "And it's obvious at least two of them have something to hide." She brought a saucer from the kitchen and poured milk into it for the kitten.

"Why do you think that?" I kept one eye on the tube. In a couple of minutes the vampire was going to rise out of his coffin.

"Take O'Hare, for one. Why was he so scared when he opened the door? Why did he try to keep us outside? And why does he eat dinner in the living room with the TV on in his bedroom? Besides, there's the evidence we found in his garbage — Galloping gophers, Lucy, turn down that TV! How can I talk?"

"In a minute. You've got to watch this. It's one of the great moments in horror movie history." I ignored her groan. "Come on, you'll love it. See, that guy doesn't even see the coffin as he comes into the dark room. Fool, he's turning his back and walking to the window." I sucked my breath. "Watch this."

Slowly, the coffin lid lifted and clawlike fingers inched through the crack. Slowly the ghastly pale creature climbed out. Slowly it stalked toward its meal of fresh blood. Then the smiling announcer interrupted to urge us to eat Sugar Yummies for breakfast.

"Guaranteed to rot your teeth or your money back," Susannah muttered. "But I've got to admit that was scary, all right. Hokey maybe, but scary. Ever seen that vampire before?"

"Are you kidding?" I snorted. "That's Morton DeKay. He's always the vampire in the old horror movies. Except the one where he's the mad scientist who cuts out people's brains and puts them into corpses."

"Sounds terrific. I can hardly wait to see that one," she grinned.

"Forget you," I snorted. "You can always go home, you know. Won't hurt my feelings."

But she stayed and, funny enough, got hooked on the movie. She didn't say a word all afternoon until Aunt Louise arrived to take her home. Pop breezed in right afterwards with Chinese takeout cartons, but Aunt Louise said they had to leave.

As Susannah was smuggling the little black cat into her jacket, I remembered something. "What were you going to tell me about Mr. O'Hare?"

"Just that — blast you, come back!" Seeing Puffin in the doorway, the kitten leaped from her arms and dived out the window.

"Forget the dumb cat," I said. "He'll come back when he's hungry. He always does. Now what about O'Hare?"

"So you've been feeding him all along." Susannah grinned at me. "I should have known. O'Hare?" She frowned over her glasses. "Just that don't you think it was strange there was a steak bone in his garbage?"

9

I didn't see Susannah again until Monday afternoon. Aunt Louise took her off to visit relatives on Sunday, and she spent most of Monday on a Science Club field trip to the Lawrence Hall of Science. I caught up with her at the bus stop after school.

"Thought you had soccer practice this afternoon," she said.

"The coach called it off because he had to go somewhere." Which was just as well. There was going to be a murder on the field if that Roger didn't quit cutting in on every ball that came my way. I never thought the day would come when I'd long to hear Knievel's two-bit bike come clattering up to school.

"Good," said Susannah. "I could use your help this afternoon. If you don't mind stopping at the post office first."

"Sure, why not?" The thought of detective work ahead raised my spirits. "What have you got in mind?"

"I thought we'd try to find a home for that abandoned kitty. The rainy season will be here soon."

"Oh great," I sighed.

House-hunting for a cat wasn't my idea of a terrific way to spend an afternoon.

On the way to my place, we stopped to buy a stamp for Susannah's letter to her grandparents, who were still in New York.

"Why bother writing them? They'll be back next week," I said as she looked through the "Most Wanted" posters on the post office bulletin board. Susannah always checks them, just in case we run into a famous fugitive somewhere. There weren't many today: two bank robbers from Florida, the leader of a terrorist gang who'd planted bombs in power plants around Chicago, a kidnapper from Oklahoma, and a murderer from Nevada. Susannah studied the posters and scribbled in her note pad.

We found the scrawny black kitten casing my door. He let Susannah pick him up, but had second thoughts when she hauled him off.

Yowling with remarkable volume for such a small cat, he tried to shred her jacket.

"See what thanks you get?" I grinned. "Hey, maybe the lady around the corner will take him. She's got so many cats already, she might not mind feeding one more."

"I've got a better idea." Susannah winked at me.

"All right!" I looked at her with respect. "The Eucalyptus Arms, you mean?" Maybe it wasn't going to be a boring day after all. "But won't Mr. O'Hare get suspicious seeing us again?"

Susannah peeled the cat off one shoulder and settled him on the other. "That's the kind of calculated risk detectives sometimes have to take, I'm afraid. Just remember to maintain our cover of being innocent kids."

The mail carrier was leaving as we reached the Eucalyptus Arms. Susannah glanced at her watch.

"He's late," she whispered. Not that anybody could have heard her over the cat.

"He always comes later on weekdays," I said. "He gets to my place about four every day but Saturday."

"That's useful information. Here, sit with me on the steps and peel our furry friend off my jacket, will you? But don't let go of him for anything. Hi," she smiled at the mail carrier. "We thought we'd sit here awhile."

"Suit yourselves." Just then the door opened and Mr. O'Hare bustled out. Fumbling with his keys, he got his box unlocked and snatched out the letters.

"You're sure that's all?" he demanded, after checking each envelope.

"Sure I'm sure," said the mail carrier. "What more do you want? You get more mail than most people as it is. Look out, you dropped one."

Susannah dived to catch the envelope as the wind tried to send it air mail to the next block. I figured this was as good a time as any to ask Mr. O'Hare if he'd like a nice cat.

"It's very affectionate," I assured him, extracting what felt like twenty cactus needles from my veins. "Quiet, too — well, usually." For the little demon was giving a pretty good imitation of an ambulance siren.

Mr. O'Hare wasn't interested in cats. Snatching the letter from Susannah, he unlocked the front door and dashed inside.

I caught the door with my foot, and Susannah followed me.

"Just as I thought, Lucy," she muttered. "That letter had an Illinois postmark. It's beginning to fit."

"Yeah?" I wasn't sure what Illinois postmarks had to do with this case. Or for that matter, a steak bone in the garbage. "Hey, where are you going?" I grabbed Susannah's jacket as she started upstairs. "O'Hare lives on the first floor."

"But Mr. Mordecai is on the second floor."

I wasn't overjoyed at the news. As I followed her upstairs, patting the squalling cat like a baby, I prayed Susannah knew what she was doing.

"Why bother with Mordecai," I grumbled as we walked down the dim hall, "if you think O'Hare — ?"

"I don't know *what* to think yet," Susannah

whispered back. "Right now I just want to check out a hunch."

She knocked at the door with the card "D. D. MORDECAI" taped to it. No answer. She knocked again.

"Not home," I said, relieved.

But something felt wrong. Even the cat had stopped yowling. The back of my scalp prickled and I had a feeling I didn't want to turn around.

"Yes-s-s?" The whisper came from behind us. "You wish to see me?"

The cat hissed as Susannah turned to face the long, thin man in the hallway.

"Yes, Mr. Mordecai." She yanked the kitten from my jacket and thrust it at him. "We brought you a cat."

What happened next took twenty years off my life. Mr. Mordecai gave a shriek that rattled the lightbulbs in the hall. "No!" he screeched, trying to scrape the cat off his coat. "Take it away! Jeremiah would never forgive me!"

"Oh, well." With a defeated sigh, Susannah unfastened the twenty little needles from Mr. Mordecai. "Guess we'll have to take him to the pound and let them put him to sleep. Sorry we bothered you."

As she turned, Mr. Mordecai barred her way.

"Well, now," he said in a soft voice that chilled me. "If this little demon is off to his death anyway, we just might try a little — er, experiment." He gazed through his dark glasses at the frantic kitten. Then before Susannah could stop him, he'd unlocked the door, snatched up the cat, and bolted inside.

"Now, we shall see how you like *this*, my little incubus," I heard him whisper as the door closed.

I still don't know what made me barge through that door. I must have been nuts.

"Give me that cat," I squeaked.

He didn't turn around, but suddenly the cat quit yowling.

"What are you doing to it?"

Slowly the long, thin man turned and smiled at me.

"Yes-s," he whispered. "It *does* like popcorn. Just like Jeremiah. Oh," he added politely, "would you ladies like some too?"

Staring past Mr. Mordecai, I saw a small blob of black fur busily polishing off a bowl of popcorn twice its size.

"Yes, thank you," Susannah answered. "After all, it isn't every day we get to eat popcorn with a vampire, Mr. Morton DeKay."

10

"Vampire? You call me a vampire?" Mr. Mordecai looked outraged.

"Well, isn't your real name Morton DeKay?"

"No," he said sternly. "My real name is *not* Morton DeKay." He walked around us to the door and, for a minute, I thought he was about to throw us out. But instead, he turned his back and opened a drawer.

"Oh." Susannah sounded crushed. "I — well, see, you look kind of like this actor who used to be in horror movies years ago. Only he was younger."

Mr. Mordecai seemed not to hear. "It is dangerous," he muttered, "to go around accusing people of being vampires." There was cold menace in his voice. "I shall have to do something about this." I wondered what he was fumbling for in the drawer.

I nudged Susannah. "We better go."

At that moment he turned. "Not so quickly, my dears," he said softly. As he smiled I saw the empty eyeballs and the pointed teeth. I shrieked.

"Easy, Lucy." Susannah's voice was shaky. "I think Mr. DeKay is just having fun — aren't you?"

He shrugged, grinning. "Didn't mean to frighten you, my dear. Not that much anyway." He pulled out the fangs and held them up for us to see. "My finest set. I wore them in *The Revenge of the Vampire.*" Setting down the fangs, he peeled a piece of white net from first one eye, then the other.

"But why did you say you weren't Morton DeKay just now?" I demanded, furious that he'd scared me so.

"I said it wasn't my *real* name. You see, the studio felt that Mordecai Fluggenheimer wasn't quite a suitable name for a vampire. And speaking of names — ?"

"I'm Susannah, and this is Lucy. We were here on Halloween."

"Yes, I remember your voices. And you" — he pointed a long finger at Susannah — "where's that catnip you promised to bring me?"

"I forgot. I'll bring it another time."

"Good. I suppose," he sighed, "Jeremiah won't mind if, instead of putting it on his grave, I give it to another cat." He reached down to stroke the kitten's chin. "Nice little fellow, but scrawny. Well, so was Jeremiah when I found him — How many years ago was it?"

He wandered into the kitchen and came back

with a can of cat food and a saucer. "Sit down and help yourself to popcorn. My friend here needs something a bit more filling."

"Mr. DeKay — "

"*Please!* Mordecai is my name now. I'd be most grateful if you'd remember that."

"But why don't you want people to know who you really are?" I asked.

He sighed and sat down near us. "Frankly, my dear, thirty-five years of fame was quite enough. Now I just want to live in peace. Nobody staring at me on the streets, nobody asking for my autograph. Nobody asking me to help them get into the movies. Above all, no reporters asking things that are none of their business."

"But I don't see why you want to live in this old building instead of — "

"Ah. Well, you see, I'm afraid I was a bit foolish with my money years back. Oh, I have enough to live on, but not in great style. And the thing I dread" — his lips tightened — "is reading in some trashy newspaper about 'poor old Morton DeKay living in poverty.' " He looked at us appealingly. "Can I trust my secret to you?"

"Certainly," Susannah said promptly. "We'll never tell anyone, Mr. De — Mordecai, I mean."

"Well," I said, "can I tell just one person — if he swears to keep his mouth shut?" I was dying to see Knievel's face when I told him what he'd missed.

"I think we *have* to tell Knievel," said Susannah.

"He was with us on Halloween, and since he's a partner in our detective business — "

"Detectives, are you? Very good ones, too, to have discovered my secret. Well, tell him then. That'll make three of you who know, plus some old friends. And that policeman, Inspector Smith, of course. I had to tell him when he came about those poor children who were poisoned. Oh," he added, "I suppose your partner was one of them. I'm sorry. Is he all right now?"

"I think they both came home today," Susannah said. "By the way, are there any popcorn balls left?"

"I gave them to the police. But I assure you, my dear detective, there was nothing in them but caramel and popcorn. The caramels came out of a bag and I cooked them well — possibly a bit *too* well. Part of them are still stuck to the pan. And if there was anything wrong with the popcorn, you'd better ask the movie theater around the corner. I got it there with lots of butter and salt, the way I like it."

I remembered the cartons we'd found, but decided I'd better not mention we'd searched his garbage. Anyway Susannah, glancing at her watch, was saying we had to go. But there was still one thing I wanted to know.

"How come, Mr. — er — Mordecai, you put on that scary scene for us on Halloween? I mean, if you don't want people to know about you — ?"

"Yes, that was a rather foolish risk to take. But how was I to know I was playing to some clever detectives? Ah, how to explain? Well, partly because I was so grieved over Jeremiah's death, I simply had to do something — well, *bizarre* — to take my mind off my loss. And then when I realized it was Halloween, I remembered how I once loved a good scare myself. And besides . . ." He shrugged.

"Besides, you just couldn't help doing what you do best," Susannah finished.

"Exactly." Mr. Mordecai grinned sheepishly.

"Okay," I said. "And I know how you made your eyes look like empty sockets. You glued those pieces of white net over them. But how did you disappear?"

He smiled mysteriously. "Ah, now. All professions have their secrets. Perhaps one day you'll tell me how you discovered who I am, and I'll show you some of *my* tricks." He bowed to us as he closed the door behind us.

"You know," I said, thinking hard as we went downstairs, "I bet he had a black curtain across one end of the room that night. It was so dark in there, remember, we couldn't have seen it. I bet he just slipped behind it when we thought he disappeared."

"That's my deduction, too," said Susannah. "But it was the eyeballs that first made me think he might be an actor. An actor would know makeup tricks like that. And I was sure of it when we found the white fabric with the holes in it and the tube of surgical glue."

"Those holes were where he'd cut out the eye patches," I reflected. "He used the surgical glue to stick the edges to his skin, didn't he? Neat trick. I'd like to try that some Halloween, only I'd need a Seeing Eye dog to get me across the street."

"You could always disguise him as a sheep if you go as Little Bo Peep again." Susannah grinned.

I ignored that remark. "I bet Mr. Mordecai doesn't see very well, even without the eye patches. He's always wearing sunglasses. By the way, why did you ask for one of his popcorn balls? The lab didn't find anything wrong with the one in your bag."

"I'm interested in something the lab wouldn't test for. But you've reminded me of another point." Susannah paused, frowning, on the front steps. "Has it occurred to you, Lucy, that the poisoner might not have doctored all the stuff he gave out? Suppose he — or she — only had enough pills for *some* of the mints or lime honey delights or whatever it was?"

I thought about it. "That would explain why the lab didn't find anything wrong with the stuff in your bag. You got an unpoisoned one."

"That's got to be the answer." She zipped up her jacket as we started down the street. "Mind if I call Aunt Louise to pick me up at your place when she gets off work at six-thirty?"

"Fine," I said. "There's a great movie on at five."

"No TV tonight. You have to type a letter on your father's typewriter. Well, don't look like that. You type better than I do."

"A letter? What do I have to write?"

"Oh, almost anything. Hmm. Let me think." She gazed over her glasses toward the hills. "I've got it: *Phone you 6:30, November 9. Be there. Important news.* That ought to do it."

"What does *that* mean?"

"Nothing."

"Then why are we writing it? And *who* are we writing it to?"

"A certain Mr. George Fritchie at the Eucalyptus Arms, Apartment 1-E."

"Apartment 1-E? That's Mr. O'Hare's apartment. And who is George Fritchie?"

"That is what I'm going to explain while we're typing the letter. Want to play another hunch, Lucy?"

11

Susannah mailed the letter on the way to school next morning. We figured it should get there the following day.

So Wednesday we raced to the Eucalyptus Arms after school. As we passed the mail carrier at the corner, Susannah pulled me to a halt.

"Relax," she said. "He won't get there for another ten minutes. Remember, act innocent. We're just a couple of kids doing nothing."

"Sure, I know." And to make us look more innocent, I popped a wad of bubble gum in my mouth and tossed her my softball.

I should have remembered what a lousy catcher Susannah is. She missed the ball, which plopped into somebody's yard. I had to crawl through a hedge after it. Unluckily, I had just blown the world's champion bubble. Next thing I knew, the bubble was caught in my hair and my hair was caught in the hedge.

"Honestly, Lucy," Susannah moaned as she

tried to untangle me. "You should know detectives never chew bubble gum on duty. Now what'll we do?"

"It's all your fault," I growled. "And if you're wrong about that George Fritchie guy, after I cut soccer practice — "

Susannah bit some bubble gum off her fingers. "Lucy, I've just got to be there when O'Hare gets that letter. Otherwise we'll never know — "

"Hi, kids." Over Susannah's shoulder I saw the mail carrier peering at us curiously. "What are you doing in that hedge?"

"Nothing much — *ouch!*" I gasped as Susannah yanked a chunk of hair free. "Just having fun. What else do kids do?"

"Oh. That's nice." Shaking his head, the mail carrier walked on.

A minute later we tore past him, pretending to have a race. By the time he reached the Eucalyptus Arms, we were standing at the door as if waiting to be buzzed in.

"Gee," I said loudly. "I'm sure they must be home."

"Ring again," he advised, setting down his satchel. "Maybe they didn't hear." He reached around us to press the bell marked 1-E.

We rang again but there was still no answer. Which didn't surprise us. I just prayed Mr. Able wouldn't hear and come to find out who was ringing an empty apartment.

“Huh.” The carrier frowned at an envelope in his hand. “Wrong address. There’s no George Fritchie here — that’s O’Hare’s apartment. Well, back to the post office it goes.”

I felt like screaming “Put it in the box!” After all my trouble typing that letter, was it going back to that made-up address in Chicago? Or would somebody at the post office remember the name Fritchie and that his face was on one of their “Most Wanted” posters?

At that moment Mr. O’Hare bustled through the door. Shuffling through the letters the carrier handed over, he demanded, “Is that all?”

“That’s all,” the carrier said good-humoredly. “Except for this one for some guy named George Fritchie I’m taking back — ”

I would never have believed Mr. O’Hare’s white face could get any whiter. “Give me that!” he shrieked, snatching our letter.

He stood there staring at the envelope, his hands shaking so he could hardly hold it. Suddenly he bolted back into the building.

The mail carrier stared at us. “Can you beat that?”

We didn’t wait to answer. Ten minutes later we burst into my apartment, and Susannah grabbed the telephone.

“Inspector Smith?” she panted. “If you want to catch one of the FBI’s most wanted criminals, the brain behind those terrorist bombings back in Illinois, listen carefully.”

* * *

I wasn't sure Inspector Smith did listen carefully. Instead of sending a squad out to break into O'Hare's apartment, he came over to my place.

"Now what's all this nonsense about terrorists?" he demanded gruffly. "Are you telling me O'Hare is really Fritchie, the leader of that gang of nuts back East?"

"Of course not." I tried to explain what Susannah had told me last night. "O'Hare didn't have anything to do with the bombings. How could he when he's hardly left his apartment since he moved in? In fact, he probably moved to California to get away from Fritchie. But Fritchie found him when he was on the run and made O'Hare hide him."

"But what makes you kids think O'Hare is hiding Fritchie?"

"It all adds up," Susannah began. "First, consider the fact that Mr. O'Hare, a vegetarian, has a steak bone in his garbage. We — er — just happened to discover that," she added hastily. "Not to mention chocolate wrappers, which seems odd for a man who never eats sugar."

"Odd maybe," growled Inspector Smith, "but I can't arrest a man for eating steak and chocolate."

"Another fact," Susannah continued. "Somebody watches TV in the back bedroom when O'Hare is elsewhere."

"Lots of people forget and leave the TV on when they go out. But suppose O'Hare *does* have a visitor who likes steak and chocolate and TV. Why should it be Fritchie?"

"Because, one," Susannah counted on her fingers, "O'Hare is terrified somebody will find out he's there. Two, he suddenly starts getting piles of mail from Illinois — "

"It's really for Fritchie from members of the gang, though the letters are addressed to O'Hare," I put in.

"Three, he buys the *Chicago Tribune*."

"So Fritchie can find out if they've caught any of the gang — "

"Four, Mr. O'Hare owns a fur cap that's twice too big for him. And somehow he just doesn't seem the type to go off skiing somewhere — besides the fact that he never goes anywhere."

"That still doesn't prove anything," said Inspector Smith. "But I'll look into the matter. Meantime, you kids quit playing detectives. You could run into bad trouble. By the way," he nodded to me as he opened the door, "did you know you've got a wad of gum in your hair?"

When the door closed, I exploded. "So he's going to look into the matter, is he? By the time he knows what's what, Fritchie will be long gone."

"Well, I guess there really isn't enough evidence for him to get a search warrant," said Susannah. "Maybe the Chicago police will come up with something to tie O'Hare to Fritchie."

I hadn't any heart to even turn on the TV.

"Huh," I snarled. "I thought at least we'd get to watch the shoot-out."

There never was a shoot-out. But the next afternoon George Fritchie was in jail.

We found out when we stopped by to visit Carla after school. Inspector Smith was talking to Mr. Able on the front steps. Breaking off their conversation, he came to meet us.

"Let me buy you an ice cream," the Inspector muttered, herding us down the block. When I started to ask questions, he gripped my shoulder. "Later," he said softly.

At a back table in Swensen's he told us. At about 11:15 that morning — "Make that 11:21 exactly," he corrected himself, glancing at his notebook — O'Hare had left the Eucalyptus Arms for his usual trip to buy newspapers. At the bus stop, a plainclothes policeman stepped up beside him, flashed his badge, and suggested they have a little talk together.

"O'Hare must have been scared out of his gizzard," I said.

Inspector Smith nodded. "He was terrified Fritchie's gang would kill him. Fritchie, by the way, is his half brother."

"I thought he might be," said Susannah. "I couldn't see how else O'Hare could have gotten mixed up with him."

When O'Hare returned to his apartment, Inspector Smith and three other policemen walked in behind him. The police grabbed George Fritchie before he had a chance to reach for his gun.

"And now," Inspector Smith finished as the waitress arrived. "What kind of ice cream will you ladies have?"

I didn't have to think twice. "Double fudge sundaes with all the extras. Well," I added as Inspector Smith checked his wallet, "we deserve some reward."

"Fair enough." Inspector Smith waited until the waitress left. "But I better warn you. You won't get any credit for your part in this business. As far as the newspapers know, the tip about Fritchie came from an anonymous phone call from Chicago. It won't hurt," he added, "if the gang thinks there's a traitor in their midst."

"That's not fair," I protested.

"Maybe not, but I'm not taking any chances with your safety until Fritchie's gang is behind bars. That's why I wanted to talk privately with you, to tell you to keep quiet about this. Think you can do that?"

"Certainly," said Susannah. "Detectives have to protect their covers. But what about Mr. O'Hare? Is he in danger?"

Inspector Smith shook his head. "As far as Fritchie or the newspapers know, O'Hare had nothing to do with his arrest. And, of course, we arrested O'Hare, too — for harboring a fugitive. That's all we've got on O'Hare right now. But I think his lawyer will advise him to tell the truth about the poisoning. Especially if the District Attorney agrees that Fritchie forced O'Hare to hide him and he drops that charge."

"You think Fritchie was really the one who poisoned the candy?" I asked, polishing my dish with my finger.

Inspector Smith nodded. "A dangerous nut like Fritchie could do anything. That's why I think O'Hare will tell the truth, rather than take the rap for him."

Susannah gazed thoughtfully over her melting sundae. "I'm not so sure about that," she said softly.

12

"O'Hare?" Knievel asked, surprised, as we finished catching him up on everything at recess the next day. "I didn't think he had that much guts."

After repeating his story to half of Washington School all morning, His Royal Highness was beginning to look as bored as his listeners. Kids, teachers, even the principal, had made such a big fuss over him, it seemed like getting himself poisoned was some great accomplishment. He'd never had so much attention, at least not without being kept after school for it. He even escaped math by claiming he felt dizzy.

"No, you goon," I snapped. "Not O'Hare. Fritchie was the one who poisoned the candy."

"But why?" Susannah propped herself against the link fence. "What was his motive?"

I shrugged. "He's a nut, that's why. Like Inspector Smith said, somebody like that could do anything."

"But why do something that was sure to bring

the cops? Fritchie may be a nut but he's not stupid. Besides, he didn't have a chance to poison that candy while we were there. Fritchie was hiding in the back bedroom when O'Hare went into the kitchen to get it."

"So Fritchie must have poisoned the candy earlier," I said.

"In that case, he obviously expected O'Hare to eat it. But why would Fritchie poison O'Hare?"

"Because he didn't trust him," I said. "He knew O'Hare might squeal on him anytime."

"Maybe," Susannah allowed. "But how could Fritchie manage without O'Hare to buy the groceries and newspapers and pick up his mail? Remember, Fritchie didn't dare show his face. Anyway, if he wanted to get rid of O'Hare, Fritchie could have found surer means than a medicine."

"Besides, how was Fritchie going to get rid of the body?" Knievel gave me a triumphant glance, then turned to Susannah. "So O'Hare did it, after all?"

"That doesn't make sense either," said Susannah. "As scared as he was of Fritchie and his gang, the last thing O'Hare wanted was a police investigation."

We stood there, thinking it over.

"But if O'Hare and Fritchie didn't do it," I said at last, "we've only got three suspects left. Uncle Bob, Mr. Mordecai, and Mrs. Sweet."

"Mrs. Sweet? Come on now," Knievel growled,

"she's a nice lady. Besides, there was nothing wrong with her cupcakes. I ate two of them. And that was long before I got sick."

"Speaking of which," said Susannah, "I'm curious about that awful taste you remember." She reached into her pocket. "Close your eyes and open your mouth. Oh, go on. Detectives have to take chances sometimes. It's just an experiment."

Suspiciously, Knievel closed his eyes and Susannah poked a blackened blob of something into his mouth. "Bite," she ordered.

Knievel's tongue worked the lump into place, his teeth clamped shut, then —

"Yeech!" He spat the brown liquid over my sneakers. "That's it! That's what made me throw up that night."

Susannah looked pleased. "I thought so. What you've just tasted, Knievel, is burnt caramel with lots of salt in it."

"Burnt caramel?" I said. "Nobody gave us caramels."

"Don't be too sure," she said. "You use caramels to make popcorn balls. And if you're not much of a cook, you might not know how to melt caramels without burning them. And you might not know better than to use popcorn with lots of butter and salt on it."

"You mean Mr. Mordecai?"

"Of course. I guessed he wasn't much of a cook from all those TV dinner and Chinese takeout cartons in his garbage. And the popcorn containers made me wonder if he'd used salted popcorn in the popcorn balls. And that, in fact, is exactly what he told us he did. Plus he'd burned the caramels."

"You know," said Knievel, "it *was* the popcorn ball. I remember now."

I felt sick. "But why did he do it?"

"Do it?" Susannah looked at me as if I were nuts. "Don't you see, Lucy? This proves Mr. Mordecai *couldn't* have poisoned the popcorn balls."

Knievel snorted. "Go on! That guy's so weird he'd smother his own grandmother."

"Knievel," I began, "there's something you better know about Mr. Mordecai. If you swear never to breathe a word — "

"Later, Lucy," Susannah interrupted. "The point is, weird or not, Mr. Mordecai isn't the poisoner. In the first place, as awful as it tasted, I doubt Knievel took more than one bite."

"That's for sure." Knievel shuddered. "One bite was enough to make me sick."

"Sorry to disagree," said Susannah, "but you'd have gotten sick anyway. The real point is that you ate it in the car. Now we weren't in the car long, and it takes a while for most medicines to act. So you must have been sick already. You threw up the popcorn almost before it hit your stomach."

So now there were only two suspects left: Uncle Bob and Mrs. Sweet.

"What do we do next?" I asked after a long silence.

Susannah didn't answer. She was gazing over her glasses with a startled look, as if she'd just remembered something. I repeated my question.

"I think," she said as the bell rang for the end of recess, "we'll start with Carla. There's something I've got to ask her."

Of all the strange things in this case, nothing was more unexpected than to find Carla playing Monopoly with Nadine when we arrived.

"Oh, good," said Nadine as she opened the door with curlers in her hair. "One of you can take my place while I go get dressed. All you need is the other railroad to win."

"Shoot," sighed Carla. "Just when things were getting exciting. Do you have to go?" But Nadine had already darted into her bedroom and closed the door.

"So Nadine plays Monopoly with you these days?" Susannah took her place across from Carla. "Funny, the only thing I thought you two would ever play together was Russian roulette."

Carla shrugged. "Nadine's not so bad when you get to know her. We were talking just before you came. She'd had a pretty hard time, her mother dying and Dad — my stepfather — always being so busy and all. That's how come she got mixed up with kids who were into drugs down in Los Angeles. And she just happened to be along when the cops arrested her old boyfriend for selling — " She broke off, looking guilty. "Please don't tell. I promised to keep that secret."

"You can trust us," Susannah said, glancing at Knievel and me for agreement.

"*We* never tell secrets," I said, reminding myself never to trust any of mine to Carla. "But you mean Nadine would be locked up right now if she hadn't pulled her sick act?"

Carla squirmed. "It wasn't an act, after all. She really did have leukemia."

"Leukemia?" Susannah whistled. "That *is* serious. No wonder they sent her to the hospital and then back home. Is she okay now?"

Carla nodded. "The doctor told her she could even stop taking her medicine."

"That's nice," said Knievel. "Look, have you got anything to eat around this joint? Otherwise, I've got to be go — "

"Have some gum." With a squelching glance, Susannah tossed him a pack. "Now, Carla, there's one question I forgot to — "

A knock at the door interrupted her, and Carla went to answer. There stood Mrs. Sweet, her hand to her forehead.

"Carla, dear, I'm afraid I can't have you up for supper tonight after all. I've got one of my awful headaches again. All I can do is take a pill and go to bed."

"Oh," said Carla, disappointed.

"But don't worry," Mrs. Sweet went on, "Uncle

Bob's gone to buy pizza. He'll be back in no time to keep you company till your folks come home."

Carla's face was bleak as she closed the door. "Please," she begged us, "will you stay while he's here?"

Susannah and I looked at each other. "Sure," we said.

"I'll phone Aunt Louise to pick me up here instead of at Lucy's when she gets off work," Susannah added.

"But you heard her," said Carla. "He's going to stay till my folks come home, and they said that would be around eleven."

"What's the matter?" Knievel looked up, interested. "Don't you like pizza? I love it, especially with pepperoni and without green peppers."

"Carla likes hers with pepperoni and without Uncle Bob," Susannah said drily. "This *is* a bit of a problem," she added, frowning. "You could come home with me, Carla, but then we'd have to get you back by eleven."

"Why don't you phone your folks?" I suggested. "Get them to tell Uncle Bob to buzz off."

Carla shook her head hopelessly. "They'll only say he's being nice to keep me company. Uncle Bob is Dad's — I mean, my stepfather's — friend, you know."

"Hmm." Susannah rubbed her chin thoughtfully. "You know, I think I know one person who just might listen to you." She went to rap on Nadine's door, then slipped inside.

A minute later Nadine burst out of her bedroom in her bathrobe. "Why didn't you say something before, you twit?"

"I did," said Carla. "But the folks never listen. Even Mom thinks Uncle Bob is just being friendly."

"Sounds familiar," Nadine sighed. "Dad never believed me either. Well, quit worrying. I'm not leaving till he arrives — and goes home." Tweaking Carla's bangs, Nadine bounced back into her bedroom.

After a silence, Carla said, "Maybe Uncle Bob doesn't mean any harm. He's really kind of nice in a way."

Susannah looked interested. "He gives you lots of candy and stuff, doesn't he? Like chocolate mint patties?"

Carla shrugged. "He likes those mint things, but I don't. I like regular chocolates better."

"I see," said Susannah. "And I suppose Mrs. Sweet bakes lots of cookies and cupcakes for you, too?"

"Sometimes." Carla began to look uneasy. "So what?"

"So nothing," said Susannah. "What I'm really interested in is those granola bars Nadine gave us on Halloween. Who made them, Carla?"

13

"Granola bars? What granola bars?" Carla asked.

Knievel and I shot a startled glance at Susannah. The granola bars?

"The ones I found under that end table by the door, of course," Knievel snapped.

"Oh those. I guess Mama bought them somewhere."

"Funny," said Susannah. "I could have sworn they were homemade. And I remember Nadine saying they were left from dinner the night before. Wasn't that the night Nadine's social worker came?"

Carla shrugged. "So what?"

"So didn't you say Nadine made dessert that night? It was those granola bars, wasn't it?"

Carla nodded, staring down at her hands.

"Granola bars!" muttered Knievel. "And here I thought only junk food was bad for your health."

Then I noticed Nadine standing in the doorway to her bedroom.

"You're wrong," she said. "I didn't make those granola bars. As a matter of fact, I made a lemon pie but forgot to take it out of the oven in time. Mom said not to worry, somebody had given her granola bars that would do. But as it turned out, Miss Ross — my social worker — brought a cake for dessert. So I set them down there to make more room on the dining table."

"And of course," said Susannah, "you'd never see them under there unless you were standing right in the doorway."

I was squirming out of my skin. "But who gave the granola bars to your mother?"

Nadine smiled grimly. "Dear old Uncle Bob."

There was a knock at the door. One of those silly shave-and-a-haircut-two-bits knocks.

"Carla, sweetie, it's Uncle Bob!"

I glanced at Susannah. "Want me to call the police?"

"Not yet. We've got to find out about the granola bars. Then we better get rid of him. We can't do anything with him here."

Knievel grinned. "You want to get rid of Uncle Bob? Leave it to me." Bounding ahead of Nadine, he flung the door open.

"Here's our pizza, Carla. Say, Uncle Bob, got any nice stories to read us? I love rabbit stories. They always make me hop around chomping on stuff."

Knievel was playing it a bit heavy, but Uncle Bob didn't seem to notice. "You mean this — this monster is staying here tonight?" His smile shrank like a balloon with a hole in it.

Nadine caught her cue. "Afraid so. His folks don't dare leave him alone in the house when they go out."

"He'll be fine," I added, "as long as you hide the matches and — "

"Quit overdoing it," Susannah muttered in my ear, adding aloud, "well, we better be going, Lucy."

Uncle Bob backed toward the door. "Now wait just a minute. Mary Sweet never said a word about *this* brat being here. No wonder she got a headache. I'm not about to — "

Knievel took the pizza box out of his hands. "Hope you told them to leave off the green peppers."

Growling, Uncle Bob turned to go, but Susannah was standing in the doorway. "Before you leave," she said, "tell us about those granola bars."

"The what?"

"The granola bars you gave Mom last week," Nadine said.

Uncle Bob looked from one to the other. "What about them? I wasn't going to eat them myself, so I thought maybe your family could use them. I hated to throw out something a lady baked for me."

I began to feel sick. "What lady?"

I didn't have to ask. All of us knew the lady was Mrs. Sweet.

"I thought so," Susannah said when Uncle Bob was gone. "I couldn't see Uncle Bob baking them. For one thing, granola bars don't seem like his thing. Besides, his garbage didn't have the kind of things cooks throw away — stuff like sugar bags and flour sacks. It just had TV dinners and liquor bottles."

Knievel set down his dripping slice of pizza as if he'd lost his appetite. "But why did Mrs. Sweet poison them?"

"You bird brain," I said, "she didn't mean to poison you and Carla. She made the granola bars for Uncle Bob."

"Any fool can see that," Knievel snorted. "But why?"

"Why," said Susannah, "has been the real question in this case all along. Why, for example, use a medicine? Sure, medicines can be dangerous, but would a killer use one? Remember, it was only Knievel's bad luck that he got an overdose by eating two or three — maybe even four — granola bars."

"Talk about getting your just desserts," I muttered.

Knievel ignored that. "You know what the medicine was?"

"I've got a pretty good idea," said Susannah.

"But first, we better talk to Mrs. Sweet. Want to come upstairs with — ?"

There was a knock at the door. Nadine opened it and Mrs. Sweet walked in. She looked grim.

"Bob's been telling me you asked about some granola bars I made. Are you children thinking I poisoned them?"

I couldn't meet her eyes. "We know you didn't mean for Carla and Knievel to get them."

"That's right," Knievel added. "You meant them for that creep, Uncle Bob."

"Bob?" To my surprise, Mrs. Sweet burst into laughter. "Now why on earth would I try to do in the only bridge partner I've got in this place? Just because he sometimes bids wildly when he's had too much to drink?"

Susannah regarded her over her glasses. "That doesn't make much sense, does it? But if you didn't poison the granola bars before you gave them to Uncle Bob, somebody else did later. So the question is, who put something into the dessert the Ables were having for dinner?"

I sucked in my breath. "You mean somebody wanted to poison Carla's family?"

"Not exactly poison. I think the idea was to get them stoned. Whoever did it thought the medicine was some kind of illegal drug."

"Like LSD, you mean?" asked Knievel.

Susannah nodded.

"But why?" I asked. "Who'd want to do that to Carla's family?"

"The real target, I think, was the social worker. And why?" Susannah looked thoughtful. "My guess is the motive was revenge. So our next question is: Who wanted revenge by getting the social worker stoned?"

I followed her gaze to where Nadine sat perched on the arm of Carla's chair.

"You take medicine, don't you, Nadine?" Susannah asked softly.

Nadine jumped to her feet. "Are you accusing me? If you think — "

"I think," Susannah said calmly, "you better check your pills to see if any are missing."

As Nadine left the room, I turned to Susannah. "But Nadine *knew* that medicine wasn't LSD."

"That is a very good point," said Susannah.

Nadine returned holding a green pillbox. "There's only three here. But I'm sure there were nine left the last time I took one. Who could have — ?"

Carla burst into tears.

14

"I never meant to hurt anybody," Carla sobbed, burying her head in her arms. "I thought those pills were — "

"We know what you thought," Knievel snarled. "You should have swallowed a few yourself, then you'd know."

"But she did, didn't she?" I asked Susannah. "Or was Carla just faking being sick?"

Susannah shrugged. "Half and half, probably. I'm guessing that when Carla realized what had happened to Knievel, she took another pill from the green box in Nadine's drawer and swallowed it. Then she played the rest by ear. Right, Carla?"

A muffled moan came from the form huddled over the Monopoly board. Mrs. Sweet knelt beside Carla and put an arm around her shoulders.

"But why?" Knievel demanded.

"Because," said Susannah, "when Nadine mentioned giving us the granola bars — you did, didn't you, Nadine? — Carla knew why Knievel was in the hospital. And when the police started investigating, she knew she might be caught — unless it looked like she was a victim of the 'poisoner,' too."

"She was dumb to leave those things sitting around after her plan bombed," I said. "Why didn't she get rid of them?"

"Ah, but Carla couldn't find them. She probably decided they'd gotten thrown out. Remember, even Nadine forgot she'd shoved them under the end table to get them out of the way. It took our sharp-eyed detective partner to spot them."

"Knievel's a genius at finding food," I agreed.

He curled his lip at me. "What I want to know is why she wanted to get Nadine's social worker stoned."

"I thought that was obvious. Want me to tell them what happened, Carla, or do you?" The hunched shoulders heaved an I-don't-care.

"Well, then," Susannah began, "Carla, of course, didn't know what those pills were she found in Nadine's green pillbox. Back then, remember, she didn't believe Nadine had really been sick. But she did know Nadine had been in trouble over drugs. So — "

"Carla told you that?" Nadine interrupted. She'd moved from the arm of Carla's chair and was propped against the dining table.

"In a way, but she didn't know much herself back then. Only what she'd heard your folks whispering."

Carla raised her head. "They — they wouldn't

tell me what really happened. Just that I m-mustn't tell anybody."

That sounded familiar. "Why can't adults just tell you the truth?" I muttered. "Usually it isn't half as bad as what you think they're hiding."

"Really." Susannah handed Carla a Kleenex. "Maybe if Carla had known all the facts, she wouldn't have hated Nadine so. But the way she saw things, Nadine was a rotten junkie her mother paid more attention to than she did to her. So when Carla found the pills in Nadine's drawer and made a wrong guess about what they were, she decided to show everybody what Nadine was really like."

"Now wait just a minute," Nadine interrupted. "That's crazy. Carla's mom is a neat lady, and she's been really good to me. But everybody knows Carla's her precious darling. I'm the one who should be jealous — Dad's nicer to Carla than he is to me most of the time."

"Maybe so," said Susannah. "I'm just telling it the way Carla saw it. Anyway, when she saw the granola bars, she thought they were the dessert you said you were going to make. And Carla had a bright idea. If the social worker got stoned on them, she'd think you did it and — "

"And send Nadine back to Juvenile Hall," I finished. "Was that the idea?"

"A pretty screwy idea, if you ask me." Knievel shook his head and helped himself to another slice of pizza. "Who'd be stupid enough to believe Nadine would do something to get herself into trouble again?"

"Besides which," I added, "Carla could have killed somebody, giving them pills when she didn't know what they were."

"You're telling me." Knievel turned a bit pale. To restore himself, he took a huge bite of pizza, green peppers and all.

"So Carla just made up the part about something tasting bitter," I said.

"That's what started me wondering about her," said Susannah. "It seemed funny Carla remembered a bitter taste when Knievel said it was salty. Then when Knievel identified the burnt caramel today, I knew she had to be lying."

"I *thought* it was strange she didn't remember anything and didn't want to talk about it at the hospital," I said.

"Me, too. At first I thought she was covering for somebody, probably Mrs. Sweet. But that didn't explain why she couldn't remember what happened to her trick-or-treat bag."

"What *did* you do with it, Carla?" I prodded her shoulder and Mrs. Sweet brushed me away.

"St-stuck it in a trash can next door," she said.

"Very smart," said Susannah. "If you'd put it in your own garbage can, the police would have found it."

"Why didn't you just get rid of the granola bar,

Carla?" Knievel asked. "In fact, why didn't you eat it instead of taking another pill out of Nadine's box?"

"But there wasn't any granola bar in her bag," I pointed out. "I barely managed to rescue two for Susannah and me from your greedy clutches. Seemed silly to give her something from her own place anyway."

"She *had* to get rid of the bag," Susannah said. "The police were interested in what was missing from it — what she'd already eaten — not what was there. And two to one, she'd at least eaten the cupcake Mrs. Sweet made with her name on it. Carla didn't want to get anybody in trouble, least of all Mrs. Sweet."

"Anybody but me, you mean," Nadine put in bitterly. "She'd have loved seeing me arrested for poisoning kids. That'd be even better than getting my social worker high."

"No!" Carla jerked her head up. "I wasn't going to let them blame you. I — I'd have told them the truth if that happened."

"Sure you would."

"I think she means that, Nadine." Mrs. Sweet stroked Carla's head. "She's not really spiteful at heart. Jealousy can make any of us think of rotten things to do. But when you cool off and have time to think it over — when you're lying in a hospital bed, say — you find you don't want to do them after all. Carla did a foolish thing in a moment of anger, but — "

"That foolish thing, as you call it, nearly got me in bad trouble," Nadine snapped.

"It's got Carla in worse trouble," Susannah pointed out. "Because the police are going to have to know what really happened. I guess we better call them now."

"The police?" Nadine frowned. "Now, look, she's just a little kid. She deserves to have her butt blistered, sure, but not to be hauled off to Juvenile Hall. She never meant to poison anybody. She was just mad at me, that's all."

"Still, Susannah's right," Mrs. Sweet said. "We do have to let the police know. But don't worry, darling. I'm sure they won't haul you off to jail."

"Really," Susannah said. "You'll probably have to go with your folks to talk to a judge. But I bet you'll get off with a lecture."

Nadine looked uneasy. "Are you sure? I don't want to come home tonight and find my little stepsister's in the clink."

Carla looked from Mrs. Sweet to Nadine to Susannah. "Call them," she said in a tired voice. "I want to get it over with."

"It'll be all right, you'll see," Susannah said.

I followed Susannah back to the kitchen to phone Inspector Smith. The desk sergeant told us to hang on a minute. While we waited, I thought of some questions.

"How come the lab didn't find anything wrong with the granola bar in your bag?"

"I probably got the one without a pill in it. Remember, there were six granola bars and six pills missing from Nadine's green pillbox. But we know Carla took one of those later, so she only doctored five of the granola bars. One for each of the five people at dinner."

"What's going to happen to Mr. O'Hare?" I asked. "Think he's going to go to jail for hiding Fritchie?"

"Now if *you* were on the jury," Susannah said, "what would you decide?"

"That he shouldn't go to jail," I said promptly. But there was still something else on my mind. "Uncle Bob," I began.

"Uncle Bob," she mused, rubbing her chin. "Hmm. I think we better get somebody to have a talk with him. Somebody like Inspector Smith — and Aunt Louise, maybe. I'll bet they can convince him to — um — mend his ways."

I could imagine how Uncle Bob was going to love having a talk with Aunt Louise. "He's probably not a bad man," I said. "Just a bit sick in his head maybe."

"That's his problem, not ours. Oh, hello, Inspector Smith." Susannah explained the situation to him. "Of course, I'm not kidding," she retorted, and after a pause, "See you later then, Inspector." She hung up the phone. "He'll be over in about an hour."

Back in the living room, Mrs. Sweet was walking unsteadily to the door. "I'm so sorry, Carla, but I really must go now. The pill I took before

I came down is starting to act. I have to get to bed before I collapse. Stay with her, will you, Nadine? She needs your help now."

Nadine scowled at Carla, but sat down on the arm of her chair. "Guess I'm stuck with you, brat."

Carla wiped her nose on her sleeve. "You don't have to stay."

"I can't leave you to face the cops alone, you dumb kid."

"It's not fair you have to miss your party. I'll be okay." Carla blew her nose and tried to look brave. "That Inspector Smith seemed like a nice man when he came to see me in the hospital."

"But — "

Susannah cleared her throat. "Maybe it'll be easier for Carla to talk to him if you aren't here. And we'll stay with her."

Nadine gave Carla a long look, then squeezed her arm. "Okay, brat, if you're sure you'll be all right. I'll go on the condition that Sherlock here stays with you. She should make you a pretty good lawyer at that."

The only trouble with being a child lawyer is that you have to get permission to stay with your client. So we went back to the kitchen to call Aunt Louise and Pop. Knievel came along to call his mom, too. Pop said I could stay if Knievel and Susannah could stay. Knievel's mom said he could stay if we could. Aunt Louise, however, was a problem.

"She says," Susannah reported, covering the

phone, "that I can't stay without an adult here. She doesn't want me to be alone after dark in a building where kids have been poisoned. I tried to explain about Carla, but — "

"Tell Aunt Louise," I said, "that we'll have an adult here to stay with us in five minutes."

I tore out of the kitchen, past the living room where Carla sat alone staring into space, and up two flights of stairs.

"Yes-s?" whispered Mr. Mordecai, opening the door.

I explained the situation.

"Certainly," he said, "I'd be delighted to regale your friends with my theatrical experiences. Providing, of course, they can all keep my little secret."

I had to think before I answered for Carla. But I decided anybody who'd kept the secret she had, could keep Mr. Mordecai's.

"Good," said Mr. Mordecai, clasping his long fingers under his chin. "And may I inquire if you young detectives solved your mystery?"

"Yes, but it turned out not to be green, after all."

"Green?"

I explained about all the green things in the case — the cupcakes, the lime honey delights, the mint patties, even the wrapping on Mr. Mordecai's popcorn balls. "But it turned out to be something that wasn't green at all. Wait a minute — " I thought of the greenish brown pills in Nadine's bright green pillbox. “Maybe it was, in a way.”

“Ah, good,” said Mr. Mordecai. “A green mystery should always have a green ending. Now I suppose we’d better be going. You don’t mind if I bring my friend along, do you?”

As he swept up the little black cat, I noticed for the first time its huge green eyes. “What did you name it?” I asked.

“Halloween.”